ARIEL N. ANDERSON

LOVE IS NO SHIELD AGAINST CRUELTY.

ENTOMBED

Cover design by Artscandare

Graphic design and artwork by Rilee Harris

eBook ISBN: 979-8-9987836-4-7

Paperback ISBN: 979-8-9987836-5-4

First Edition: February 2026

10 9 8 7 6 5 4 3 2 1

❀ Formatted with Vellum

National Suicide Prevention Lifeline:
1-800-273-8255

A portion of the net royalties from all Ariel N. Anderson titles are donated to the American Foundation for Suicide Prevention

PROCEED WITH CAUTION

This is a retelling of the classic ballet *Swan Lake*. The stories, in the original adaptation and in this one, are inherently ***tragic***.

There is no on-page sexual content in this novel, but it still contains mature themes.

Content Warnings Include: graphic birth, violence, death, miscarriage, and themes of sex.

"Even lizards are not immune to poon."
-My husband

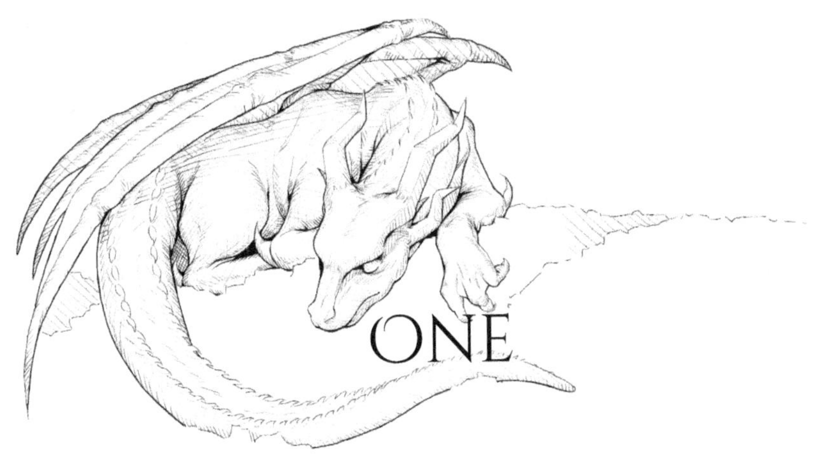

ONE

Before the silence, before the fire and the screams, the dragons lived in great prides that spiraled through the mountains like living storms. They were communal creatures bound by ancient bonds older than stone. The young slept piled upon one another in warm mounds of wings and soft bellies, purring in low, rhythmic hums that echoed through the caverns like song.

Dragons did not fear the darkness—they illuminated it. Their fire was not only a weapon, but a hearth, a beacon that lit their homes and warmed their eggs through the long winters.

In those days, every pride had a Matriarch, chosen not by strength, but by wisdom. It was said the Matriarchs could feel the emotions of every dragon under their care, a tether woven from flame and instinct, so that no hatchling was ever truly alone.

When dragons took flight at dawn, they did so in great

sweeping arcs, wings overlapping like a tapestry across the sky. Their bodies cast shadows large enough to paint entire valleys in dusk, but their hearts were gentle toward their own.

The humans never saw this. They saw only the shimmer of scales from afar and imagined greed. They saw great wings blotting out the sun and imagined conquest. They watched flame dance across the horizon and imagined destruction.

And because the humans never saw the tenderness, they convinced themselves it did not exist. So when the Dragon War came, they only saw it as destroying monsters.

HE REMEMBERED THE SCREAMING. Not dragon screams. Not the deep, thunderous roars of his kind. That was low and ancient. It was the breath of the kings of the mountains.

No.

The screams he remembered were the screams of the humans. Shrill and chaotic and frenzied with fear. But what followed was much worse.

It was the cries of the dragons dying.

He was young when it happened. Far too young to understand war and suffering, but old enough to vividly remember it all. The sky was black with smoke the day his kind fell.

He remembered his mother's golden scales. Her regal, vast wingspan covered his small body as she stood with the other mothers to defend the young. She whispered in their ancient, draconic tongue to run if they fell. And when they did, she begged him to save himself. To be brave.

He ran. His small wings were barely strong enough to carry his body, but he forced them to. He ran until the ground no longer shook from battle, and he ran until the mountains flooded with the blood of the dragons.

He ran until silence was the only thing left. He hid, curled into a small crevice of fallen rock, letting out terrified cries for help in his tongue, hoping another would find him, but they never did.

The humans called it a victory. Their laughter echoed off the charred cliffs as they carved weapons and armor from their scales. They celebrated as they hung bones on their mantles as trophies.

He survived, but only just.

For years, he did not speak, did not cry, did not show his flames. But when the world forgot the language of the dragons, he did not.

Time forced the slaughter of the dragons into stories for the humans. But for him? It hardened him. He grew into the exact thing the humans thought his kind was. He grew into the exact thing they slaughtered the dragons for: a savage beast. The last of his kind, left with nothing but fire and fury in his heart.

He could not weep for what was lost, so instead, he vowed he would never *lose* again.

He began hoarding.

In a cave carved deep into the tallest, jagged mountain in the region, his treasures grew vast and mismatched. Gold coins. Goblets inlaid with precious gems. Pearls and shells.

Senseless trinkets. Cracked instruments. Children's dolls. Jewelry.

He did not know why he kept these things, only that once he found something, he could not let it go. He could not discard it. It was *his*.

The humans had taken everything from him, and so he took from them. It wasn't about hoarding petty human wealth—he had no use for such trivial things.

To lose things meant he was weak, and he could not allow himself to be weak.

THE LAST DRAGON lived alone for nearly a century.

He did not fly far from his cave. He only hunted when necessary. Only glided through the sky under the cover of thick clouds.

Sometimes, when the anger hit him, he would fly over the human villages late at night, eyes narrowed, watching them huddle near their fires because they feared the dark.

But he *was* the dark.

Still, he left them alone, though it was hard sometimes.

He did not speak the human tongue, nor did he understand it well. But he understood well enough to know what they were.

They killed not just the dragons, but each other. He watched them burn their own villages in civil war. He watched men hang thieves in the square. He watched mothers abandon their babes for being born with imperfect skin.

The humans killed for land. They killed for power. They killed for superstition. They killed for sport.

And still, they called the *dragons* monsters.

The last dragon no longer roared. Instead, he growled. It resonated deep in his chest when the rage swelled, but no one was left to hear it. No one left to understand the pain and the agony that lingered there.

No one left who would even care.

Many years into his solitude, at the turn of the century when the humans celebrated another rotation around the sun, he lay curled up in the furthest corner of his hoard, his massive tail wrapped around a broken harp, stray coins clinking as they rubbed against his hardened scales.

He thought about fire. Not the kind in his heart nor the kind in his throat.

He thought about the fire that was meant to warm. The soft kind. He remembered a time when he was, too, a young hatchling, sleeping in piles with the others like kittens. Their tails and wings would tangle together and they would coo and purr at the comfort it brought.

He remembered hearing his mother hum ancient songs in the dragon language as she turned eggs in the communal nest.

Dragons were not meant to be lonely creatures. They lived in large prides, filled with tens of families. He had siblings, not just from his own mother, but from the others, too.

It had been so long since he had felt the heat of another

body beside his own. He almost forgot how it felt, for none of that heat remained, not even a single ember.

Now his heat was meant only to destroy. In wiping out the monsters, the humans made him into the very thing they feared.

He was no longer young, but neither was he old. His body was strong, his flame hot, his instincts apt. Yet in all those years of solitude, he had grown into something unrecognizable even to himself.

There were nights when he woke snarling from dreams of flame, confused and fearful of the silence in his cave. He would rise, prowling and hungry.

Not for food, but for sound. For life.

There was none. Only stone. Only treasure.

And rage.

Always rage.

THE STARS of the night bled over the ridge as he descended into the forest.

His wings beat the wind into silence—into submission. Each gust sent pine needles to the ground below. Birds scattered. Deer fled. Even the mountains seemed to hold their breath.

He had not hunted in two days. Not a hunt with prey—that was daily. But the hunt for *things*. It was time again for him to take from the humans as they took from him.

He landed deep in the forest, where things lie mostly

untouched by the unclean human hands. There, overgrown and forgotten, was an ancient temple from a time long past.

From a time when the humans believed in gods.

The ruins were covered in moss and bird droppings. The once grand spires were blackened and dirty from neglect. Though it had been abandoned for a long time, he could still smell the humans. Their scent sat in the air like rot.

He approached the temple, the ground beneath him cracking under his weight. His sharp claws scraped against the old stones as he climbed the steps, his tail dragging like a flail behind him. He sniffed the air first, his nostrils flaring in disgust at the scent of man.

He could still see their footprints on the stone. He followed their path until they reached an ancient altar of worship. And there, a small glimmer rested on the smooth rock.

He sniffed again, his chest rumbling on the exhale.

Gold.

With his body too large to move any further into the temple, he extended his long, forked tongue to wrap around the golden trinket. He pulled it toward himself and out of the temple to examine it in the moonlight.

It was a statue the size of a human newborn, in the shape of a woman. Time had worn away the finer details, but the shape of her delicate hands remained.

He observed the hands for a long time, and a part of himself, deep in the recesses of his memories, ached for the humans to understand him.

And then, as quick as that thought came, he growled before grabbing his treasure with his ruthless claws and carrying it back to his cave. His hollowed-out cathedral of stone filled with treasures that meant nothing to him.

Just a pile of useless, meaningless things.

He harshly threw the statue into a pile of gold coins before laying beside it, curling his tail around the base.

His treasures were all he had to protect.

He was alone.

Always alone.

TWO

IN HER VILLAGE, order ruled above all else. Order was peace. Order was safety. Order was absolute.

Justice. Punishment. Law. These were the doctrines of her people.

Elowen knew better than to ask for softness, or to ever expect it. She moved through the narrow stone streets like a slip of shadow, her body too thin for the coarse fabric that hung from her frame. Her long dark hair, usually braided to keep it neat for the Council's scrutiny, often escaped in loose strands that brushed her hollow cheeks. Her blue eyes, striking even when lowered in obedience, noticed everything, even the things she was punished for seeing.

Her bones pressed gently against her skin—the sharp angles of collarbone, the pronounced curve of her ribcage, the thin wrists that looked as though the slightest pressure might snap them. She, like so many in the village, bore the unmistakable signs of hunger: pallid skin stretched too tightly over delicate structure, faint tremors in her hands when she worked too long without rest, a weariness that lingered in the hollows beneath her eyes.

Her physical fragility did not dim her presence, it sharpened it, making her stand out like a single fragile flower growing through cracked, darkened stone of the houses that were filled with darker silence.

The cottages were lined up in narrow, uniform rows like teeth clenched in a jaw. No one planted flowers in their windowsills. No one hung paintings in their homes. No one loitered. Laughter, if it even existed at all, was hushed behind thick curtains and quickly silenced. Families kept to themselves and taught their children obedience before they even uttered their first word.

Expression was weakness in her village. Questioning the rules set in place by the Council was treason. And kindness? Kindness was foolish, dangerous, and forbidden.

Elowen had learned these things as a young girl, but she ached to be different.

She was always too quick to comfort. Too slow to judge. Too eager to shed a tear when a thief lost a hand or question why the poor and sick were given less food during the harsh winter months than the healthy, even though they were the ones that needed the nourishment the most.

Elowen knew that softness was equivalent to danger.

Like her father, she grew up to become a healer, though the townspeople trusted him more, for he was both a man and more experienced in the art. Her father was quiet, firm, and always obeyed the Council's orders without question.

His touches were clinical, and his words were few.

Elowen, by contrast, was gentle. She hummed quietly to herself when she crushed herbs. She would let her cold palms linger on a child's feverish brow for a bit longer than needed. Her heart ached when a woman would come in seeking a pain remedy for bruises shaped like her husband's fist.

There was a part of everyone in the village that tolerated her for this, as it was human nature to seek comfort, but that was all they did: *tolerate.* They did not accept her, nor like her, nor trust her.

But she did not care. Or at least, she tried not to.

Elowen had but one freedom, and it was the forest.

Beyond the high iron gate of her town, past the guard's torches and the stone walls, lay the beauty of nature. This is where Elowen found peace and serenity in her rigid world. Even the light seemed softer there, filtered through a thick canopy of trees that changed with the seasons into vibrant shades of yellow, orange and red before falling lifeless in the winter—only to turn green again.

She visited the forest often, under the excuse of gathering roots and other ingredients. The Council approved of her collecting, so long as she returned before dark and her satchel was inspected upon return.

Everything she brought back became the property of the town, and so however much she might have wanted to, Elowen was not allowed to have *things.* No one was.

Deep in the forest, far from the paths laid by men of the past, there was a lake. It wasn't large, but it was wild, natural, and real. Cupped between moss-covered hills, surrounded by soft meadow grass and floral shrubs, the lake reflected the beauty of the sky every day and night in a way no mirror ever could.

Animals, too, found peace there. Deer would come for a

refreshing drink while foxes played in the brush. A crane would show off its beautiful balance, while fish bobbed at the surface of the water, waiting for insects to land.

The lake was where Elowen was allowed to feel. She was allowed to unbraid her hair and decorate the locks with flower buds. She was allowed to draw shapes in the soil. She was allowed to sing, even if she didn't know any songs.

Here, the world was gentle, and Elowen could be gentle with it.

Her village trusted the forest as much as they trusted her, and that was very little.

Long ago, in a time before anyone in her village was born, dragons once lived in the mountains and hunted in this forest. It is said that their blood soaked into the roots and deep into the stone.

Her village said the forest was cursed by their blood, but Elowen did not feel that way.

It felt like the only place in her world that wasn't.

Still, she was careful. She never strayed too far from the lake, and certainly not any deeper into the forest. She was a healer, not a fighter, and Elowen did not want to put herself in danger, forced to defend herself while alone.

One day, while foraging near the lake for mushrooms, she saw something strange.

A trail of thick, dark, fresh blood in the grass.

Something within her stirred, and her healing nature overrode her caution, compelling her to follow.

The blood cut through the soft grass in uneven strokes, as if something was wounded and attempted to stagger to safety, only to collapse every few steps. Elowen crouched, her satchel thumping softly against her hip as she followed the trail.

It never occurred to her to turn back, so she continued forward, even though the sun was already dipping behind the trees and she knew she must return home before dark.

Her heart raced as she followed the blood trail. Something within her wanted to believe there was more to the woods than her small village knew—that magic still lingered there. That she wasn't the only one who felt like the silence between the trees wasn't as empty as it seemed.

Then, near a small clearing, she saw it: a corpse.

Not of a human or a dangerous beast. But of a goat. A large one, well-fed and plump. Or at least, it was before its belly was torn open, leaving behind thick claw marks raked across its hind. Flies had already begun to gather at the wounds. Elowen exhaled softly, and knelt beside it. She brushed a hand over the stiffened leg.

As she stroked the strawy hide of the goat, her fingers grazed over the brand burned into the rear near the tail. She recognized the marking well. Livestock from her village, belonging to an old man with no family. The council kept him well-paid in exchange for keeping them well-fed. An even trade in their eyes, while half the town went to bed every night with the sharp ache of hunger in their bellies.

The goat must have escaped its pen and found a bloody fate here in the woods. Elowen eyed the claw marks again. Not from a wolf, as the marks were too wide. Not from a bear either, as they didn't hunt in that part of the woods. The marks were also too deep to have been from a falcon or eagle.

Something else downed the poor animal. Something big.

Night began to fall, and Elowen needed to return home before she was punished for being out past curfew. Before something returned to finish off its meal.

Elowen stood. She didn't hum or think, just hastily walked home with a stirring, unsettling feeling in her gut that she was no longer alone in the forest.

BY THE TIME she returned to the stone walls of her village, the guards had closed the heavy iron gate. But Elowen was used to slipping through the bars when the guards were lost in conversation amongst themselves.

Once back inside the walls, she could freely walk, no longer afraid of being caught out after dark, though curfew quickly approached. Elowen tightened her thin shawl around her shoulders and made her way to her father's cottage.

It was small, like all the others. Even smaller, maybe, because the front entry functioned as a small store when the townspeople needed remedy for some wound or ailment. She shared a single bedroom with her father, sleeping on the floor on a mattress she made herself out of worn-out clothes and feathers she'd collected over the years during her ventures into the forest.

When she finally pushed inside the weathered door to her home, her father sat at the small table near the fireplace, poking the glowing embers with an iron rod. He didn't glance up when she entered, just let out a gruff sound of acknowledgement that she had returned.

"Find anything?" he asked.

"No, father," she said.

He grunted. "Useless girl," he muttered. Not with any cruelty, but with exhaustion. The Council always requested something new from her father. A new potion or salve or tea. They ran her father ragged with work sometimes, and it was Elowen's job to make sure the ingredients stayed stocked.

Sometimes, though, like today, she'd return with nothing, and her father quietly feared it would be the day the Council ran out of patience with him.

Elowen didn't flinch at her father's words. She never did. She simply sat her empty satchel down on the floor near the door and moved to a small basin to wash her hands. The cold water ached in her bones and bit at her skin, so she joined her father at the fire to dry and warm them.

That night, they shared a dinner of stale bread and water-thinned gruel. Flavorless. Hard to swallow. But it was all they had, and both she and her father knew better than to complain.

Complaints about such things were forbidden.

After she washed the plate and bowl they shared for dinner in the same basin she washed her hands in, she crawled into her flat, uncomfortable mattress on the floor, and pulled her shawl tight around her to try and hold in the warmth.

She lay awake near the window, staring at the silver moon and stars from a world far beyond her own.

One day, she thought, she'd like to be closer to the stars.

Her mind began to drift back to the goat and the claw marks, thinking hard about what beast could have caused such an injury.

She remembered a weight in the air she'd never felt before, but quickly corrected herself. She was surely just imagining things.

Still, she couldn't shake the feeling that something had watched her there in the forest, and maybe even hunted her.

Elowen closed her eyes, forgot about the goat, and dreamed of wings bringing her high above the clouds to touch the stars.

THREE

HE SMELLED her before he saw her.

She did not smell of manflesh—not entirely, at least. Her scent was slightly different. The humans always reeked of fear and sweat and the acrid tang of metal they worshipped, a stench that clung to them like rot.

But she smelled of crushed herbs and damp soil, of river reeds warmed by sunlight. There was another thing too, buried deep beneath the surface of her skin, a faint sweetness like the sap from the trees his mother once gave to the hatchlings as a treat during cold seasons.

It stirred a memory he had long since buried: the warmth of a nest, the brush of gentle claws turning eggs, the soft hum of contentment that filled the caverns before the war.

He inhaled again, slower this time, and found something else threaded through the layers of her scent. A subtle, trembling note: fear of her own world. Fear of cages and rules and silent cruelty that radiated from her village like poison.

It confused him, intrigued him, angered him. She smelled like two things that could not coexist: softness and suffering.

He was already hidden when she arrived, curled into a rocky ledge high above the glade, just out of sight. His wings were tucked close to his side as he pressed himself into the cold stone to make himself smaller and unseen.

He had barely clawed into the goat when her smell filled his nostrils.

A human woman stepped into the meadow like she had walked the path a million times. The trees seemed to part for her. The silence seemed to welcome her.

He narrowed his eyes with distrust, ready to strike at any moment.

She was slender, cloaked in dirty, old fabric. Her hair was in a messy, intricate braid and her cheeks were flushed with a soft, natural sweat. Her shoulders were strong and unafraid, posture far too regal for the rags she wore as clothes.

She had seen the body of the goat, but she did not seem to fear the thing that had injured it.

He watched her and waited, expecting a recoil, a scream, a whispered prayer to the old gods. But she did none of those things. She approached the goat slowly and kneeled next to it.

Her hands were delicate and did not tremble. She examined the wounds carefully, examining the depth of the gashes and felt over the hide.

She was not frightened. She was *curious*.

His nostrils flared as she stood, slowly, turned, and left.

No panic. No fury. No fear.

Just a slow, deliberate, and quiet return to her village. He followed her there. Not close, but just enough to keep her in sight.

She moved like someone who was familiar with these woods. She stepped over roots without looking, avoided thorn bushes with ease, and touched leaves softly as she passed. She even picked a small handful of berries and shoved them into her mouth as she walked.

He tracked her to the edge of her village, where tall stone walls broke the serenity of the forest and tainted it with the stench of human. She slipped through the iron gate and vanished behind the stone.

He could not follow further, so he turned back silently and returned to the goat. He approached the corpse, huffing smoke out of his nostrils to ward off the flies, and resumed his meal. The meat was cold and unsatisfying.

But it lingered with the smell of her.

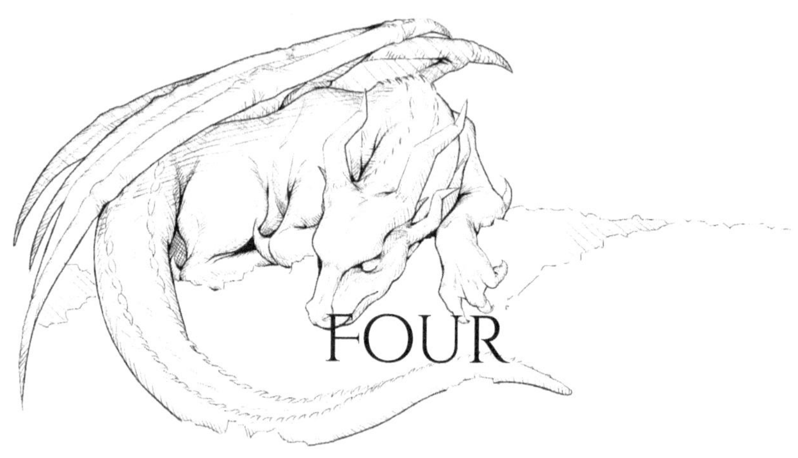

FOUR

Elowen woke to shouting.

It pierced through the morning fog, rough and furious, bouncing off the stone walls outside her window. She sat up quickly, brushing her loose hair from her face, and peered out the narrow slit of glass.

Half the village had gathered near the center square. Both Elowen and her father quickly stepped outside to witness the scene.

At the center stood the owner of the goat she had found in the woods. He was red-faced with anger, pointing a crooked finger at a cluster of the poor gathered in an alley between two houses. His coat hung loose on his thin, hunched frame, and his accusatory voice cracked like a whip through the silence of the crowd.

"Thieves!" he roared. "Dirty, useless thieves! You think you can take from me without consequence?"

The group of the poor did not answer him. They never did. They looked like old leaves waiting to be crushed by a boot; their eyes stayed low and their shoulders were hunched inward. Boney hands of mothers clutched their children with malnourished, extended bellies, trying their best to shield them from the man's cruelty.

Elowen's chest ached for them. She knew it wasn't them that stole the goat. She had seen it with her own eyes, felt the farmer's brand under her own fingertips.

But the poor—who were always cold, hungry, and sick—were convenient scapegoats for any misfortune that befell the people.

It hurt Elowen's heart in silent ways. She could have spoken up in defense of the poor, but then the Council would demand proof, or worse, they'd punish her for not telling them about the injured goat sooner.

So she said nothing.

The goat farmer raged for several minutes more. Spit flew. Fists clenched in accusatory ways. He called them thieves and expletives. He demanded justice.

The three members of the Council arrived in dark, thick, wool coats, with faces hidden by masks of ancient bone. Their voices were quiet and clipped, and their judgement was swift.

"There is no evidence of theft," they determined. "Dismissed."

The goat farmer sputtered with disbelief, but he did not argue. The Council's word was law.

Elowen let out an exhale of relief. No punishment today, and for that, she was thankful. A rare occasion where blood did not spill after their judgement.

The Council believed in correction only through suffering. Only the most heinous crimes were punishable by death. Otherwise, they believed in retribution and justice through spilled blood and lifelong scars.

Elowen though, she believed in prevention. And that's what made her different. But charity was considered a sin. Food, shelter, and health was something her people had to earn.

Elowen never believed in those things, and ached for a world where her compassion was cherished, not punished.

Later that day, she left her father's cottage with her satchel slung across her shoulder, and no one questioned it. She was the healer's daughter who braved the forest. The strange one that wandered, but they tolerated nonetheless, because she brought them valuable ingredients that benefited the town.

Elowen noticed immediately that the forest felt more tense than usual. Not necessarily unsafe, but different. The light filtered through the trees the same way that it always did, but the branches lacked birdsong.

She gathered what she needed, listening to the forest around her a bit closer. She foraged until her satchel was heavier than normal, making up for returning empty-handed the night before.

When she approached the lake, it was as quiet as ever. Reeds and wildflowers ringed the edges, billowing softly in the wind. Elowen crouched and uncorked her water skin, dipping it into the shallows to gather some freshwater.

She wiped her brow with the back of her sleeve, and the smell of her dirty garment filled her nostrils. She turned up her nose. She was alone, and in no danger of anyone seeing her immodesty, so she stood and pulled off her dirty dress. She stepped into the lake and used a rough stone to rub the dirt out of the fabric. The water around her turned a muddy brown from the filth, but her garment emerged clean. She set it on a rock to dry, and dipped her head under the water to clean her own skin and hair.

Water was carefully monitored in her village, so bathing was few and far between, alternating her water rations with her father so he could bathe as well. It was normal for her people, the dirt and the grime, but she loved the feeling of clean skin.

Once Elowen was satisfied with her bath, she emerged from the water and laid on the edge of the lake, fully naked, exposing herself to the sun as it dried her skin. It was a moment of peace.

When she was dry, she redressed and sat on a large rock. She found a long, thin stick in the dirt and stirred the algae absently, watching dragonflies skim across the surface of the water.

One landed, and a quick, silver-scaled fish darted upward and snapped it from the air.

Elowen laughed quietly at the splash, and watched the fish chase the insects as she hummed to herself. No song in particular, and no notes that made sense, but she allowed the sound to flow from her throat freely.

She looked up at the sky, and she exhaled with mist in her eyes.

FIVE

THE LAST DRAGON returned to the lake before sunrise, staying hidden in the trees along the northern edge of the water. It was a dangerous thing to stay in one place for so long, and yet, he had.

He convinced himself that it was to make sure the humans did not come to this place, searching for the missing goat, but part of him just wanted to see the woman again.

When she emerged from the opposite side of the woods, her hair was loose around her shoulders and her face was flushed prettily with sunlight.

He simply watched her. Watched her drink, watched her bathe, watched her go about her little rituals: collecting water, digging in the dirt, laughing at the fish.

Laughing.

The sound startled him. He had not heard such a thing in decades. The last time he had, the laughter had been laced with malice and triumph.

But hers? It was soft, real, and joyful.

He shifted slightly in the shadows at the noise. She did not notice.

She began to hum then, and he closed his eyes to listen. The notes made no sense, and the tune seemed to chase no melody, but there was somehow still something...*soothing* about the sound.

He tried to memorize a pattern that was not there.

He had never trusted humans—not after what they did to him, to his kind. This human girl was no different. He did not trust her, and every instinct he had told him to move quickly and scorch the clearing with her in it. To finally reveal to the humans that he still existed. That they did not wipe out the dragons as they once thought. He wanted to instill the fear in humans that they made him feel as a hatchling.

And yet still, this human did not feel like the others. She was not armored, and she did not carry a weapon. Instead, she wandered, she listened, and she gathered what she could while respecting the peace of the forest.

He watched her until the sunset began to paint the sky in warm shades of orange and pink, and until she stood again. She brushed grass from her skirt and tucked her water skin into her satchel before turning back to the woods.

He stayed where he was until her scent faded into a memory. Only then, did he move to return to his cave.

When he was there, one treasure in particular caught his eye.

A golden statue of a woman—the one with gentle hands. He stared at the figure for a long time, tilting his head from side to side as if expecting the human girl to emerge from the gold.

She did not.

Because she was not a treasure. She was a human. And humans were dangerous and destructive.

Even the gentle ones. Even her.

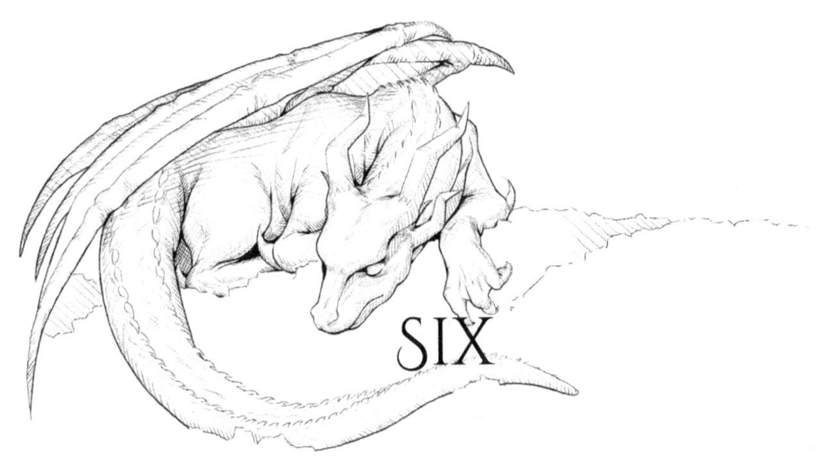

THE COUNCIL HAD ISSUED new orders that morning. Stricter rations, earlier curfews, more contraband searches. They said it was for safety. But to Elowen, it was nothing more than a noose around her neck.

Worried that they would restrict her permission to go into the forest, Elowen slipped away from the town even earlier than normal, looking for something, *anything* useful in the forest that would make the Council feel that her trips were still valuable to the village.

She slipped through the trees before the sun had risen, her satchel empty, her steps quick. She followed the familiar trail that led to the lake, the morning light shimmering off the surface when she finally arrived. Dragonflies flew erratically like hot embers across the water as she knelt to fill her waterskin with the crisp drink.

That's when she saw it: something shimmering, half buried in the reeds, just at the edge of the muddy shore.

Her hands reached for it before she had time to think,

fingers brushing the dirt and grit away from the object, and lifting it from the soil.

Not a stone. Too heavy. Too smooth in some places and too jagged in others. Triangular. Thick at the base and tapering to a fine edge like an arrowhead. It was black as coal, but when the sun hit it just right, it glowed with a rich gold.

And more than that, it felt warm, like fire burned under the surface. Alive, almost.

Elowen turned it in her hands, examining it from every angle, smelling it—biting it even, frowning when she could not recognize the strange object.

What are you?

What creature could have left such a thing behind? She knew of no such animal.

This was...something else. Something unknown. The Council had drilled into her people long ago that the unknown was dangerous, and so she should have felt afraid.

Instead, she felt like she'd found something she wasn't meant to see, but was somehow meant to keep. A secret. Something all her own. A memory no one could steal from her.

Knowing she could not take it home with her, Elowen dug a small hole back into the edge of the lake where the mud would keep it safe.

She covered it with dirt and marked it with a flat, pale stone. Not a grave to be forgotten, but a treasure to be found again.

FROM THE COVER OF TREES, the dragon froze. His eyes were fixed on the shape in her hands, and his body was coiled tight in frustration.

Fool, he thought.

He had not noticed he lost a scale, for it happens so rarely. They typically only shed when he was wounded or strained, but he was an old creature, and his scales had hardened with age, shedding occasionally to grow anew.

He usually crushed them, or buried them, or even swallowed them to keep them out of the ever-greedy palms of the humans.

He must have lost it the last time he was here, distracted by the very same woman who now holds a piece of him in her hands, curiously examining it like it were a fine gem.

The last dragon watched as the woman stood and looked around, gaze drifting through the trees. Her fingers slightly tightened around the scale, but she made no move to run. She did not scream. She did not call out for help.

He waited for that moment though, his body tight and ready to pounce the second she bolted for the village. Yet, just when he thought she might move, she sat instead, setting the scale in her lap as she dug in the mud for roots and bugs.

When she was done for the day, she reburied the scale and marked it with a stone before returning to her village.

He did not leave the shadows until long after she was gone and the night was deep. When he finally approached the marked spot, he didn't immediately uncover it.

He stood over it. Stared. Felt something unfamiliar stir in his chest.

Not rage. Not suspicion.

Something far more dangerous: curiosity for the strange woman with gentle hands. For her obvious attempt to keep his scale a secret from others.

The dragon considered her for a long time before sticking his nose into the dirt and unburying the scale. He wrapped his tongue around it and swallowed it like he'd done many times before.

As soon as it slithered down his throat, something else in him stirred. For a fleeting moment, he wondered if she would be saddened to return to her secret to find it gone.

And with that thought he put a name to that feeling: guilt.

THREE DAYS PASSED before Elowen was allowed to return to the forest. Two of the Council members fell ill within hours of each other, vomiting up their supper.

They accused their kitchen maid of poisoning them, of treason. When Elowen and her father purged the sick from them, they promptly ordered the young girl to be tied to a post in the town center, where she was given ten lashes.

The Council must have felt merciful that day.

Elowen and her father were given no acknowledgement or thanks for helping them through their illness; not that they expected it.

Their stores grew thin, and Elowen itched to return to her lake. She wasted no time when her father told her to return with a full satchel before dark.

It was already midday, so her time grew thin. She rushed into the forest and headed straight for the lake. When she reached it, she flung off her satchel and began digging for the strange stone she found the last time she was there.

Elowen swore she knew where she had buried it. Even remembered marking it in case she forgot. The lake's edge was dotted with small holes from her digging, but Elowen's secret was nowhere to be found.

Something fractured in her tender heart at the loss of her stone. In a world where she was not allowed to keep things for herself, she had one small secret. She did not know if it was human or animal that took the stone from her, but it hurt all the same. A single tear fell from her left eye, and she wiped the other before any more could fall.

Once again, Elowen had nothing.

And so, with only her own thoughts to fill the silence in her heart, she searched the dense cluster of trees near the lake for useful plants.

While there, she lingered a bit longer near a thorny rose bush, feeling the soft petals between her fingertips. Elowen loved flowers, but only ever got to enjoy them in secret here in the quiet forest. These roses were undisturbed and grew large and free in the rich soil.

Oh, how Elowen wished she could take one home with her. Something beautiful to wake up to. A sign of color and life in the uniform blandness of her village.

But she also knew such beautiful things deserved better than to be hidden in shame, which is what would happen if she tried.

With her satchel full and her heart aching, Elowen returned to her village. She sat wordlessly in front of the small fireplace as she crushed herbs and sorted the other ingredients into small jars.

Her eyes grew tired as the night went on, and she had a fitful sleep, waking before the sun. Her back ached from the floorboards, and her bones felt heavier than usual. She stared at the thatched ceiling for a long time, watching a beam of moonlight slip slowly across the room, soft and cold. It reminded her of the lake. The hush of it. The way her reflection always looked gentler there, like the water had a way of softening her features, easing the edges of her weariness.

There was no easing anything in the village.

When she stepped outside with her basket in hand, the village was already stirring with sharp voices and sharper footsteps. No one greeted her. They rarely did, unless it was to ask for a remedy or to comment on the dirt beneath her nails. She walked quietly, like a shadow in her own life, trying not to draw attention.

She took the long path out of the village, down the worn trail that led into the forest. The trees welcomed her with their usual rustle, the canopy reaching overhead like arms shielding her from the world behind her. And yet, even among the trees, she couldn't shake the weight in her chest.

It was the stone. Its absence. Its disappearance felt like a theft of something sacred, even if it had only been hers for a fleeting moment.

She didn't know why it hurt so deeply—only that it did. Perhaps because it had felt like proof that something more existed. That the world wasn't just rigid spines and cold glances and rules. That magic still lived somewhere.

That wonder was not dead.

She didn't want to return to her village with just plants.

She didn't want to return at all, if she was honest. She imagined staying here in the woods, building a little hut by the lake, living off herbs and fish and rainwater. She imagined stringing flowers into her hair every morning, letting the world see her soft and unhidden.

But dreams like that were dangerous.

So, she walked.

She picked herbs with practiced fingers, her mind elsewhere. She stopped by the rose bush again, hesitating before reaching out to pluck a single bloom. But her hand stilled in the air. *No. Not here. Not yet.* She let the petals brush her skin, let the scent cling to her fingers, and then turned away.

When she reached the lake again, the light was turning gold. She sat in her usual spot—her *secret* spot—where once her strange little treasure had been buried. She traced the shape of the soil with her hand, half-hoping it might reappear like a miracle, but the earth was undisturbed now.

Elowen leaned her head back and closed her eyes.

For a long while, she said nothing. Thought nothing. Just listened. The lake lapped against the shore. Wind shifted the grass. Birds flitted between branches in quiet, feathered arguments.

Then, finally, she whispered into the silence.

"I don't want to go back."

The words felt heavier than she expected. She wasn't supposed to say them. Not even to herself. To doubt the order of things was to invite suspicion. To dream of anything outside the stone walls of the village was to court danger.

But the truth sat in her chest like a weight she could no

longer carry. She hugged her knees to her chest, blinking back the sting in her eyes.

After a while, the restlessness of the previous night caught up with her, and she mindlessly fell asleep at the edge of the lake, listening to the rustling of the leaves in the wind and the chirp of birds hiding in the trees.

She rested for several hours, her body jolting awake with the fear that she had slept through the day and into curfew, but the sun was still high in the sky, on its way down to painting the blue above in shades of purple and orange.

Elowen rubbed the sleep from her eyes, and when she oriented herself once more, the wind carried the soft scent of something...floral into her nostrils.

There, lying next to her, was a rose.

Her breath caught. Not a wildflower or one of the stubborn water lilies that cling to the far edge of the shore—but a perfect, deep red rose, life still clinging to its petals.

Her fingers brushed the stem. It had no thorns, as though whoever left it had thought to remove them before placing it so carefully.

Elowen glanced around, heart fluttering with a mix of wonder and fear. She was alone. No footsteps marred the damp soil. No voices called out from the trees. There was only the steady rustle of wind in the leaves and the rhythmic lapping of water greet her.

But she knew, deep down, this was no accident.

She lifted the rose to her nose and inhaled. It smelled real. Living. Freshly picked. She smiled, small and uncertain, the weight of it blooming warm in her chest.

"Thank you," she whispered, her voice barely above the

wind. She didn't know if they could hear her, but then, something in the trees shifted, and birds shot into the sky from the disturbance.

She watched for as long as she could, the rose resting in her lap, waiting for the gifter to emerge from the trees.

Nothing appeared.

But Elowen could not find it in her heart to leave the rose at the lake. Despite the danger of getting caught with it, she carefully placed the bloom and stem under the warm softness of her breasts, hoping to both conceal it and keep it close to her heart.

And from deep in the forest, unseen golden eyes closed, pleased.

EIGHT

ELOWEN'S STEPS slowed as she approached the lake's clearing, sunlight breaking through the trees in long, slanted shafts of gold.

Something pale caught her eye, and she froze.

There, nestled right where she always sat, next to where she had once buried that shimmering black-and-gold mystery, was a new gift.

It was a stone. Smooth and polished, pale as moonlight, veined with thin streaks of lavender and rose. She bent to pick it up, brushing dirt from its surface with a gentle thumb. It wasn't something that could be mistaken for natural placement. It had been set there. *Left* there.

Her heart beat harder.

She glanced around the lake's edge, scanning the trees for signs of anyone. But the forest was quiet.

A small smile curved slowly across her lips.

She knew it wasn't a coincidence. Something—someone—had left this for her. Not a villager. No one from her home would bother with such a strange, lovely token. This...felt different.

It felt kind. It felt thoughtful, as if it was chosen specifically because she thought it would be pretty.

She sat carefully beside the water, her knees folding beneath her skirt. Holding the stone close, she let her fingers run over its surface again and again, like it was something sacred.

In a world where she wasn't allowed to own anything of beauty...someone was giving her gifts.

The ache in her chest loosened just slightly.

She gathered herbs slowly, savoring her time here. The lake, the flowers, the trees; this was the only place in the world that didn't ask her to change. Here, she didn't need to hide her gentleness. She didn't need to pretend she didn't care. She could just *be*.

She had just finished clipping a cluster of wildflowers when she felt it: a presence.

Weight in the air, like a storm fast approaching. Elowen turned, and froze. Across the clearing, half-shielded by a dense cluster of trees, stood a creature of legend.

Its body gleamed like burnished obsidian in the filtered light, dull-pointed scales layered like impenetrable armor. Its wings were folded carefully at its back, the membranes stretched carefully along elongated bones. Horns jutted from its skull in perfectly symmetrical angles. The light shifted and caught its intelligent eyes. Gold. Bright, brilliant, ancient gold cut with deep black vertical pupils. The world narrowed to that gaze. Its tongue flicked over rows of jagged teeth as it studied her in silence. Smoke coiled faintly from its nostrils. Each talon that jutted from its four legs sank into the earth with immense weight. Sharp. Deadly. The tail, many times longer than a human was tall, sat behind it, motionless.

It was enormous, so large that her eyes struggled to take it all in at once, but it was coiled low to the ground as if trying not to frighten her.

It was a *dragon*.

Elowen's breath caught. Her knees locked.

It didn't move closer. It didn't growl or bare its teeth. It simply...watched her.

Elowen's hands trembled around her stone, holding it close to her heart as if it were the most precious thing in the world.

She should have been afraid. Terrified. Screaming.

But she wasn't.

Even with her heart pounding, even with every instinct telling her she was staring at death incarnate, she felt no fear.

Only wonder.

The dragon blinked slowly. Elowen dared a step forward. Then another. "H...hello."

The dragon tilted its head, as if trying to understand. Or maybe...as if *listening*. Elowen swallowed hard. It did not offer an answer, but the air between them felt *charged*, like a struck bell still humming.

A sudden low growl trembled through its chest. The sound rolled across the clearing like distant thunder, making the air vibrate. The movement was not a threat, but an instinctive recoil, a memory of fear that lived in bone.

When she continued to step closer, she watched the body of the beast tighten as if ready to strike. She quickly took a step backward and carefully sunk to her knees, the stone still close to her chest, as a gesture of safety and submission.

"I won't hurt you," she whispered.

The dragon growled, low and quiet in warning. Its tail curled protectively near its haunches, but its gaze never wavered. Heat radiated from it in slow waves, distorting the air the way flames warped the horizon. Its breath rolled across her skin like warm wind from an ancient forge, carrying the scent of smoke.

And Elowen understood, it was afraid, too. Not of her, but of what she might *do*, what her people had done before. This creature, this majestic, powerful thing—was a survivor. A relic of the old world. Unwelcome. *Misunderstood.*

Just like her.

She watched the dragon's eyes flicker to the stone in her hand, and she suddenly had a foolish, wild thought, that the dragon had left it for her, along with the rose still hidden in her home.

She didn't know how long they sat there in silence. Minutes, maybe hours. But eventually, with the sun lowering, she stepped back, placing the stone back where she had found it.

The dragon followed her movement with his eyes but didn't pursue.

"I can't bring it, but I'll come back," Elowen said softly, her voice barely a breath. "And I won't tell them. I promise."

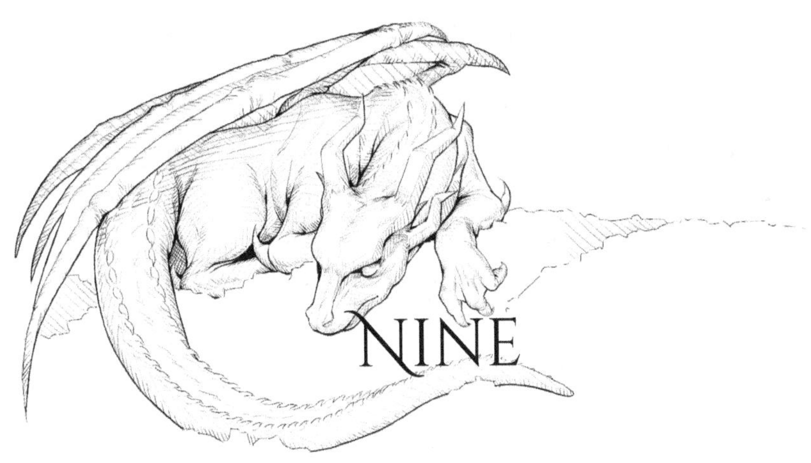

NINE

He knew it had been a mistake. He was too close. Too curious. Too trusting.

Even now, nestled deep within the forest, he could feel the echo of her gaze etched into his scales like a spear logged between his scales. A *human's* eyes were wide, soft, unafraid.

He'd seen that look before, long ago, just before the sword came down.

He paced the perimeter of the trees, restless. *Fool,* he snarled inwardly. He hadn't meant for her to catch him.

He was only meant to watch. Like he always did. From a distance. Unseen, unknown. That was how he had survived when the rest of his kind had not. But the girl with the lake-colored eyes was not like the rest, and that frightened him more than a sword. Not because she was different, but because he *wanted* to believe in that difference.

He shouldn't have left her gifts. The rose. The stone. And yet...watching her cradle them, cherish them, had twisted something tender and long-dead inside him. Something he could not name.

He ground his teeth together, breathing hard through his nose. Smoke curled around him as heavy as the shadows. The trees trembled faintly with the rise of heat in his skin.

Let them come, he told himself. *Let them see what's left of the dragons.*

He would raze her village if he had to. Turn their crops to ash. Crush their stone houses beneath his claws. He'd promised himself, long ago, that he would never let another human take anything from him again.

And now he'd shown himself. For *what*? A scrap of kindness from a strange girl with trembling hands?

He waited, crouched and coiled like a predator, golden eyes unblinking as the hours bled together. But no torches came. No men with spears. No screaming. Just...birdsong. Dawn.

A trick, he thought. *They wait until she returns. Until I come again.*

The hours crawled. Hunger gnawed at him, but he didn't leave. His wings twitched. His tail lashed slowly through the loose dirt. Still, the forest remained untouched by human footfall.

By midmorning, he felt the buzzing in his nerves. An old instinct. The one that always came before betrayal. The itch in his scales that told him when death was coming.

He snarled low in his throat.

But then, just as the sun reached its zenith, he heard the crunch of leaves. He stilled. There. A figure stepped into the clearing.

She walked slowly, carefully, as if sensing something unseen. Her satchel was slung over her shoulder, but she made no move toward the usual clusters of herbs. Instead, she moved toward the water's edge.

No weapons. No soldiers behind her. *Alone.*

That made no *sense.* It *defied* sense.

Humans were cruel. They were greedy. They feared what they didn't understand, and then they destroyed what they feared. That was the law of the world. The way things had *always* been.

And yet he could smell no blood on her. No steel. No scent of deceit. Just crushed herbs, meadow dew, soft soap, and the faint salt of old tears.

He did not move. He stayed shrouded in the trees, breath caught in his throat.

She smiled at the lake. He narrowed his eyes.

Why? Why hadn't she brought them? Why hadn't she screamed? Why did she...sit?

He watched her hum under her breath as she began picking wildflowers from the water's edge. She braided a few together in a clumsy, uneven circle and held it tenderly in her hands as she waited.

For *him,* he foolishly assumed.

He could not bring himself to come out of the shadows for fear of what might come next. Instead, he watched her until the sun began to fall. She would return to the village soon.

And all the time, she sat alone. Unarmed. Gentle.

He saw a wetness on her cheeks as she set the flowers on a rock and returned home.

By the time he returned to his cave deep in the heart of

the mountain, the sun had died behind the horizon and the stars had crawled across the sky to take its place.

He curled into the far end of the cave, wings folded tight, the walls of his hoard glinting dimly in the dark. But none of the gold, none of the jewels, none of the treasures that once filled him with comfort brought any peace tonight.

For the first time in years...he felt uncertainty. He hated it. And yet he would be at the lake again tomorrow.

Just to see if she came back.

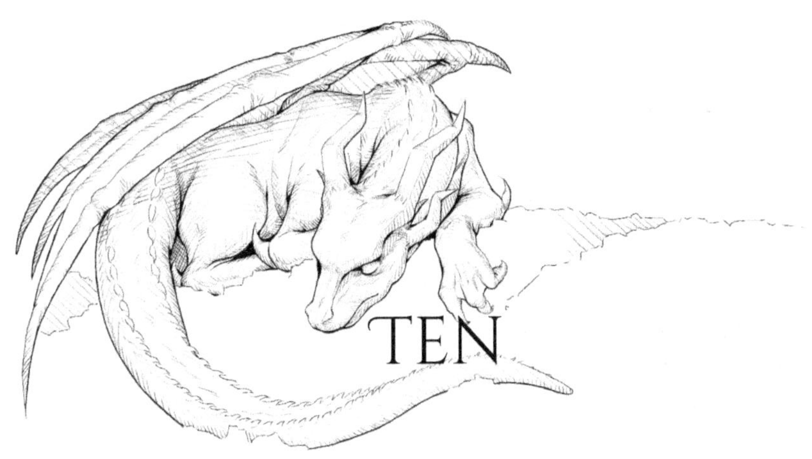

TEN

ELOWEN WOKE before the sun had finished rising, heart fluttering like a trapped bird. It wasn't fear. Not exactly. It was something else—tighter. Stranger.

Hope, perhaps.

She didn't tell her father where she was going. He hadn't asked, because he already knew. As long as she returned with a full satchel and didn't invite the Council's wrath, she could vanish into the forest for hours without question.

The morning was heavy with fog, and when she came into view of the lake, the dragon was already waiting.

Her steps slowed the moment she spotted the curve of his massive black shape, still as stone on the far side of the water. He hadn't hidden himself this time. He stood tall in the clearing, wings slightly folded, tail curled around his body. He was staring at something.

Her breath caught when she realized *what* he was looking at.

The flower crown she had left—forgotten beside the smooth stone she liked to sit on—was carefully placed in front of him now. Not trampled. Not burned. Not discarded. *Moved.* Deliberately.

He must've touched it. Held it.

She stepped forward, slowly. The dragon's massive head turned, tracking her movements. She could see the tremble of power in his limbs even at rest.

Elowen took a shaky breath. "You came back," she whispered.

He tilted his head, as if listening.

"I wasn't sure if I would see you again," she admitted, stepping closer. "But I...I wanted to thank you. For the stone. And the rose."

He blinked once, silent. No movement. No growl. No fire.

"I made this for you," she said, voice quiet as wind over water. She knelt to pick the crown from the dirt and held it up with both hands. "I don't know if you'd want it, but...it's the only thing I know how to make that's pretty."

The dragon watched her. No comprehension flickered in those golden eyes. She smiled softly. "You don't understand, do you?" She took another careful step forward, keeping her hands raised. He didn't move. "You've given me gifts. I want to give you one in return."

Still no response.

Swallowing, she stepped within reach. Her heart thudded so loudly she was sure he could hear it. *Gods, he's massive.* His body radiated heat like a forge. His breath smelled of ash and hot air. Up close, his scales shimmered black and gold, layers upon layers of ancient armor that no man could pierce.

She reached up, slowly, trembling fingers brushing the side of one great, curled horn.

The dragon did not flinch.

Her chest ached at the gentleness in that stillness. "Thank you," she whispered, rising on her toes and slipping the flower crown over the horn.

It hung there, awkward and small against the magnitude of him. And then the dragon lowered his head further.

It wasn't submission. It was *acceptance*.

Elowen, barely dared to breathe, but reached up again—this time to gently touch the edge of one thick scale near his jaw. Her fingertips pressed lightly to the warm, textured plate.

Immediately, she recognized the texture. It had been a scale she had found buried in the dirt that day, and the creature must have taken it back after she found it out of fear she would tell someone.

She moved her hand slowly across his scales. He made a sound, softer than a growl, and went still.

For a moment, neither moved.

Her touch was feather-light, the kind given to something sacred. Her hand lingered just a heartbeat longer, then fell.

"I don't believe you're a monster," she said quietly. "Not like the stories say."

Elowen stepped back, placing her hand gently over her chest. "I'll come again tomorrow," she said, voice barely more than a whisper. She turned, slowly, and began walking back toward the tree line.

Behind her, the dragon lifted his head fully, the flower crown still resting crookedly around his horn, catching the morning light.

ELEVEN

IT WAS NOTHING BUT *WEEDS*, the circle she had put around his horn. It was twisted together by clumsy hands. Wilted at the edges. The petals smelled of morning dew and faint skin oil. Human-made. Imperfect. Fragile.

The little circle of flowers sat lopsided atop his horn, and though he could shake it off with a single twitch of his head, he didn't.

He did not move at all.

Her scent still clung to his scales. Her warmth lingered like sunlight where her fingers touched his jaw. So *gentle*. No one had touched him in a hundred years. Not without hatred. Not without fire or steel.

And no one had *given* him anything.

He stared at the lake, at the ripples where her footsteps disturbed the bank. The flower crown weighed nothing, but his chest felt tight, as if the bones inside him were expanding.

She should not exist. She *should not* be able to look at

him without fear. Should not *want* to give him something. She should not hum. Should not smile. Should not speak to him.

He did not understand it. He did not *know* what to do with it.

All night, he sat there—immense and silent—unable to leave the lake's edge. Not even to return to the mountain and the comfort of stone walls and gold hoards that never betrayed. He could not go, because he was afraid.

Afraid that if he moved, the crown would fall. That if he left, this...*strangeness* inside him would go with it.

He remembered *everything*. The first time he heard a human scream. The way their arrows pierced his mother's flank. The last time he saw his brothers fly. The ache in his throat as he roared their names for the final time.

A phantom ache pulsed along the old wounds beneath his living armor. He remembered the humans chanting around the firelight as they told stories of the slaughter.

He had watched them grow old and weak and angry. Watched them build cages around themselves and call it civilization.

And now, one of them gave him flowers.

It should be *laughable*. Insulting, even. As if such a thing could change anything. As if kindness could undo a hundred years of *grief* and *cruelty*.

But when she touched his scales, she did not flinch, nor curse him, nor beg him for favors.

She simply said, *thank you.*

The dragon closed his eyes, and for the first time in decades, the fire inside him flickered not with fury, but with confusion.

He *knew* she would not keep returning. She will break, like all humans do. She will tell someone. Or they will follow her. Or she will disappear.

They *always* disappear.

But still...

He pressed his tail more tightly around himself and rested his head atop it, careful not to disturb the crown. The petals brushed against his brow with every breath. It was unbearably soft.

He wondered, not for the first time, what her name was. He wondered what would happen if he asked, not that he could speak her language to do so.

And then he growled low and long into the ground, ashamed of the thought. It is *dangerous*, this wondering. This yearning.

Still, he did not remove the crown.

He let it stay as the stars rose, as the night stretched long and cold around him. And though hunger gnawed at his bones, though his hoard lay unguarded in the dark, he did not leave the lake.

Because the human girl gave him something that could not be bartered or stolen. Something she had made *for* him. Something that was truly *his*.

TWELVE

THE LAST DRAGON hated the humans.

The sound of their voices still haunted him in sleep. Their laughter. Their screams. Their hymns to false gods while they wiped out his kind. He remembered all of it. Every cruel thing that fell from their lips, even if he did not have the knowledge to understand the language.

He had seen them rip scales from dying dragons and wear them as armor. He had watched them hammer bones into weapons, boasting of their power. He had seen them light fires in the nests of unhatched eggs and heard the hatchlings shriek as fear stole air from their tiny lungs.

He had hated the humans for so long, that hate had become him. It was in the marrow of his bones, in the flames behind his teeth, in the sharpness of his claws. He lived on that hate. He thrived on it. It constantly reminded him that he still existed, and that something of his kind still remained.

And yet...that human girl defied it all. She looked at him

as if he were something equal, not a monster to be feared. She spoke to him softly, brushed his scales with her equally soft fingers.

She should have run, or called for her kind to strike him down. Nothing about her made sense, which made her the most dangerous human of all, and it terrified him.

Because he began to wait for her. He began to hope she would return. He began listening for her footsteps near the lake in the early morning and paced as he waited for her to emerge from the tree line.

His thoughts wandered when they shouldn't. Even now, resting among his hoard, surrounded by glittering things, he was not thinking of gold.

He was thinking of her. Of her voice. Of her tenderness when she dared touch him, and her thoughtfulness of making him a crown of flowers. How small the little gift was, and yet how immense it felt to be given it.

The dragon shifted, the piles of gold sliding against themselves like sand. He stared into the shadows of his cave as he tried to recall the sound of her voice saying anything that might have been her name.

He did not think she had ever given it, and that disappointed him.

Names had power once. In the old days, when dragons ruled the skies, to know a name was to know the soul. Names were carved into the hatchling's shells as they emerged.

But the last dragon could not remember his.

He could not remember the strength in the name his mother had given him. Those memories were fog and fire, wings and blood.

He had forgotten it, and the thought hollowed him.

To have no name was to be void of a part of himself. To be nothing. To drift through life without meaning.

Perhaps this is another reason why he hoarded things—to fill the emptiness his own name could not.

But now...he wanted *hers*. He wanted to shape her name in his mouth to see if the sound could warm him in the cave's endless cold. He wanted to see if it was as gentle as she was.

He wanted to keep it as one of his treasures, not to own, but to cherish.

He growled softly to himself, shaking the thought away. This was madness. Sentiment. Weakness. Stupid human things.

He rose slowly, stretching his wings until they scraped the cavern roof. Gold and bone glimmered in the half-light. The flower crown still hung crookedly from his horn, wilted now, yet he could not bring himself to remove it.

He turned toward the mouth of the cave and looked down the long slope of the mountain toward the forest below. She would be there again. He *knew* she would.

And when she came, he would continue to ache for the sound of her name. If he ever learned it, he would keep it in his fireheart where it could not be stolen or forgotten.

And maybe then he would finally know his own.

THE SUN DIPPED behind the trees, casting gold across the lake's surface. The girl stood at the edge of the water, and he was already there, waiting for her.

He sat near the treeline with coiled limbs tucked under him like a cat, his great wings folded neatly at his sides. She stepped closer to him, her eyes catching on the flower crown still dangling from his horn.

"Hello again," she said, but he did not understand it.

His golden eyes followed her carefully and curiously, but he did nothing. He remained so still that if not for the rise and fall of his chest, one might mistake him for a creature carved from stone.

"I wish I knew what you were thinking," she said between them.

She turned away for a moment, kneeling to collect roots from the bank. She glanced back to find the dragon had shifted, his massive head tilted a little farther down.

He was trying to listen. A low and rumbling sound came from him, resonating in her bones, and he subtly nudged his head forward, bidding her to keep talking. He could hear her heart hammering in her chest, but she did not seem afraid.

She lifted the handful of roots and pointed to them. "We use these when a child gets a rash," she said.

The dragon gave no answer, but he made that sound again, and she continued on. He didn't know the words she spoke, not in the strange, sharp tongue of humans. Her sounds twisted in ways no dragon's throat could mimic.

But still, he *listened*.

And though he did not understand her words, something in her voice pierced the old, scarred part of him that remembered what warmth felt like.

He did not have a name, but if he did, he would have given it to her, if only to hear her say it back.

HER VOICE CARRIED on the wind, soft, uneven, and strangely comforting. She talked, but never expected an answer. When she paused, the dragon made gentle sounds to get her to continue, and she always did. That alone made her different, because she somehow had learned to listen where others would have ignored. Humans always demanded, but she never took what he was not willing to give.

She was a small creature, in the way all humans were, but there was something so beautifully odd about her. She did not carry weapons, nor did she cast frightened glances over her shoulder at him, nor did she reek of false courage or deceit.

Because of these things, he always followed her, from a safe distance of course. He curled low against the earth, but the ground did not tremble with fear, and neither did she. The forest knew him now, and so did she.

Though he could not understand all of her words, he understood her voice; the tone of it, the cadence. He had managed to collect a small vocabulary of the human tongue. The worst of them, he had learned, was *home*.

Because when she said *home*, she left. It always happened before the sun dipped behind the horizon, and he felt himself dreading those moments, for it meant he was alone again, if only for the night.

As that time approached, she knelt by the lake's edge, her hands wet and red from pulling herbs. Her brow was smudged with dirt, and the hem of her dress was soiled with mud. The wind stirred her hair as she looked up at him in quiet acknowledgement.

He let out a low rumble back. Not a warning, no, never with her. It was a sound closer to...need. A way of asking her to stay without words. His golden eyes narrowed in concentration as he watched her gather her things, trying his best to form words his beastly throat was incapable of.

"You know," she said, rising to her feet with her satchel on her shoulder, "I can't keep calling you *you*. Or *dragon*. It doesn't feel right."

Dragon. He understood that word.

She took a tentative step forward, and though he could hear her heart quicken, she didn't look afraid. His breath warmed the air between them like a hearth, and his eyes, the color of molten precious metal, locked on hers.

"I think I should give you a name."

Name. He understood that word too. His head tilted in curiosity. *What is it? What is she saying?*

"A name is..." she drifted off, "well, it's important, I think. It makes you unique. Like me," she lifted her hand to her chest. "My name is Elowen."

Name. Elowen.

The dragon lowered his head, slowly, and exhaled deep, misting over the soft grass. She smiled at him, like she knew he was listening intently.

"You like to hoard things, like the crown I gave you. It's

wilted now, but you haven't shaken it off. You're greedy in your own way, for meaning, aren't you?" The dragon blinked once. "*Midas*," she finally said. "Like the king with the golden touch. But I don't mean it like a curse, not in the way the old stories tell it. To me…it means you see value where others don't. You…treasure things. Even me."

There was a stillness between them, and then she lifted her hands to her chest again. "Elowen," she said, then gently touched the end of his snout. "Midas."

He moved then, not away, but closer. He curled his massive body around her as if she were something fragile and precious. He kept one golden eye trained on her, like he was guarding his most beloved possession. She stood in the curve of his body, awed and quiet, and rested her temple to his jaw.

And though he could not say her name, he etched it into his soul, alongside the one she had given him.

THIRTEEN

MIDAS.

The name lingered like warmth beneath his scales. It sank deep into the marrow of his bones. For centuries, all he had been was the last. A relic from a time long past. The rage hidden within the hollowed mountain.

But now he was *Midas*, and he thought it was the mightiest thing he had ever heard. She had given it to him with meaning and care, alongside her own name.

They were no longer human and dragon, siren and beast. She was *Elowen*, and he was *Midas*.

The moment she left after naming him, he returned to his cave like waves crashing into the ocean. Not for hunger or fear, but for need.

The treasures of his hoard glittered against the flames in his throat. He stood amidst the piles—jewels the size of apples, crowns of silver, countless coins of gold. Midas snarled low in his throat. Nothing, *nothing*, felt worthy of her.

She had given him a name, and he had nothing of equal value to return.

He dug like the mad beast the humans thought he was, clawing through dead, lifeless trinkets he had gathered over lifetimes. He crouched low, his wings folding in tight, his breath heaving with fire simmering low in his throat. He wanted to burn it all, because none of it was worthy.

Then, he remembered how sad she had been when she returned to the lake to find his scale missing from its hiding spot.

Perhaps a part of himself was the only thing he could give her in gratitude. Midas circled himself several times, turning this way and that, trying to determine which scale would be best. The ones on his tail were too small, the ones from his snout too worn.

Finally, he chose a scale from his chest, ripping it from its place with his sharp claws. It was a dangerous thing, to expose such a vulnerable part of him, but the only thing he could give her of equal weight.

He returned to the lake long before the sun would rise, arranging the gift on the soft grass among wildflowers.

Elowen came, as he knew she would. She hummed quietly as she stepped through the tree line, and found the scale within seconds. Her footsteps stilled, her humming faded, and Midas nearly shook with anticipation.

She knelt in the flowers, brushing her fingers over the scale before lifting it. The veins of gold shimmered under the sunlight. A gentle smile crossed her face as her thumb rubbed the grooves. She looked up at Midas and sighed, standing slowly.

"Thank you," she said to him. "It's beautiful, but I can't take it home with me."

Home, she said while shaking her head. Midas thought on it for a moment before he understood; she could not bring it with her to the village.

She spoke again, almost pleading, though not with him. She was pleading with the rest of the world. "I want to keep it with me, but I cannot keep it safe. They will take it."

Midas leaned forward, trying to understand. He didn't comprehend the words, but he could see the way her hands clutched the scale only to hold it out to him solemnly, as if letting go of something precious.

When she turned her head over her shoulder to look toward her village, her body dropped with defeat. Midas stared at her, carefully observing her body language. As he looked, something tightened in his chest. It wasn't the old ache of rage, but the burn of grief for her.

She was afraid of them. Afraid of the humans. Afraid of what they did to beauty and kindness and joy. She might be the only human who could see the rest of them for what they were: savages.

Elowen stepped forward and placed the scale atop his tail that was coiled around itself near his wings. "You must keep it safe for me. It is a part of you, and they don't deserve to take it."

Midas did not breathe. She gave it up, gave it back, for safekeeping, because she trusted him. He shifted slightly, then leaned forward to nudge her gently with his snout.

Midas was an intelligent creature, and knew that he could no longer bring Elowen things that the other humans could take from her. Trinkets would not do. She needed more.

As he watched her sort through the wildflowers around him with her shoulders hunched forward in concentration, he noticed the way her bones protruded against her skin, and the way her old dress barely held onto her thin frame. Her fingers trembled slightly with exhaustion, and there was a hollow sharpness in her cheeks. Her collarbone jutted against her chest, and he was now keenly aware of how the effort of fatigue laced her movements.

She was withering away. Starving. He growled, a deep, resonating sound from deep in his chest. It pulled Elowen's gaze to him, and without a warning, he moved away from her and into the trees.

He did not wait to see the confusion on her face, nor did he try to explain with their limited understanding of each other. There was no time for any of it, only the need to fix what he had missed before.

The hunt was brief and swift. He returned to the lakeside with a large buck between his bloody teeth. It pleased him when he saw Elowen was where he had left her, and he dropped the deer gently near her knees.

When she didn't move, he nudged it toward her with the claws on the edge of his wings. He was not waiting for praise or thanks, he was waiting for her to eat. He could not bear the knowledge that she was starving, because any semblance of her suffering felt like his own failing.

There was no time for her to gather wood for a fire or for her to clean the meat herself, and so Midas butchered the buck with his claws. He made a messy job of it, but the best of the meat was separated from the carcass, and he cooked it with the fire from his own throat. When he was done, he deposited the meat in front of her again and watched with intense eyes.

She ate the meat slowly at first, but the more bites she took, the quicker she ate. The juices of the meat coated her lips and chin, and when she had finished everything her stomach could hold, she looked up at Midas with a new sparkle in her eyes.

He'd fed her well, and it pleased him, so he would continue.

AFTER THE BUCK, Midas made it a point to bring Elowen something to eat every time he visited her at the lake. When her lips curled around a fresh fig or juicy meat, he watched; not with hunger, but with a strange, tight satisfaction. It was like the crunch of bones beneath his claws after a hunt. It was like the clinking of gold beneath his body when he fell asleep on a pile of coins in his hoard.

Elowen, he decided, was part of his life now—hunger and hoard. Not something to be consumed, but something to be kept. Something to protect. Something to adore.

And that meant proving himself.

Not just with food, of course. Anyone could hunt. Even the weakest of males could find meat. But Midas was not anyone. He was the last of his kind, and that made him mighty and strong. He was a prince of ashes and king of the skies. Born in fire, forged in ruin.

And he must prove it, but not because she asked him to; Elowen asked for nothing—but because something in him *ached* to give. To show her the worth of all the things he had, and the worth of the dragon he had become after all this time.

Midas' hoard began to change.

Gone were the days of hoarding for *himself*. Now, he found things and wondered if *she* would like them.

A silver bell. A silk ribbon. A polished stone the color of a winter sky. Each offering carefully placed near her side of the cave.

She had seen none of it yet, but he built the shrine to her deep in his cave where he could keep it safe from human eyes. One day, when he was ready, he would show her all of it.

Even though she could not fully understand what it meant to him when she smiled at his gifts, he craved that soft, stunned gratitude. He did not hoard gold for wealth, or jewels for beauty.

He hoarded symbols of worth. He did not save these treasures for her because she needed them, but because *she* was the treasure, and he hoped these things would help her to see it one day.

He could not ask her to stay with words, and so he

asked her in actions—in gifts. In the steadiness of his presence beside her. He would give her safety, and warmth, and anything else she lacked with the humans.

Midas did not believe she realized it, but Elowen did not belong in that cruel village among the humans.

She belonged with *him*.

FOURTEEN

MIDAS CROUCHED deep in the bowels of his cave, tail curved protectively around the cache of gifts he had gathered for Elowen. He stared at the flower crown she had once given him. It had long since withered, nothing more than dry straw, but he had kept it anyway.

Midas looked down at the claws, massive and gleaming, made for survival, not for gentleness. Not suitable for holding something so small and fragile as her.

Elowen had touched him gently. Taught him words. Smiled when she saw him. Midas ached to give her even more of him, something real she could see and touch and that could touch her back without fear of harming her. Something that did not have to hide in the shadows of the trees.

Midas moved deeper into his cavern, into the very heart of the cave, where the warmth of the magic of ages past beat like the heart in his chest.

His wings were nervously curled into his sides, and his breath was low and heavy. Midas trembled with doubt as he called on that ancient magic of the dragons.

He wanted to be closer to her, and once the thought sparked in his mind, it could not be extinguished.

Midas closed his eyes. Pain lanced through his spine, his large, strong bones folding in on themselves. His skull reshaped to be narrower. The teeth in his jaw receded into his gums until they reformed mostly blunt. His scales drifted apart and then back together again, like a cracked stone expanding and contracting with the seasons. His wings grew smaller, but they did not shed, nor could he lose his tail, which curled behind him and whipped side to side through the pain. His horns still protruded from the top of his head, and he grew...hair. Long, unruly, black as a starless sky as hers was, for it was the only shape he knew; the only beauty he had ever learned to admire.

When he opened his eyes again, he stood shakily on two legs. Tall, trembling, sweating. Naked except for the jagged patches of scales across his center and shoulders that he could not change. His claws were still there, sharp at the end of shaking human-sized fingers.

He was...small. So very small.

It was horribly uncomfortable. Unnatural. And yet still, he hoped Elowen would find it suitable—that she would understand why he did this.

Midas tested his smaller wings, which ached because they were so heavy compared to his smaller, human-sized back muscles. It took all of his effort to move his feet from the ground, and he could only manage to fly for a moment before he stumbled to his boney knees, landing in a pile of gold coins which seemed to mock him in this form.

He felt weak and unsteady, but he did not try to shift back. Instead, he started toward the lake.

He found her there, of course, but he could not bring himself to reveal his new form to her. She stood in the sun, humming softly as she examined the leaves on a creeping vine. Lost in herself, she did not hear his approach.

Midas looked at her, not as a beast, not as a shadow, but something as close to equal as he could manage. He stepped nearer, his clunky human-like feet making more noise than he was used to. She turned, hearing him at last, and when her eyes met his, she gasped, dropped her satchel, and took a purposeful step back.

Midas tried to form words in his strange human-like throat, but it came out as a rumble, a growl. He tried again, wheezing out a sound.

"Mm–Mi–Midas."

Elowen went even more still than she was before. She stared at him, wide eyed, though not with fear. It was something else, but he could not put a word to it.

Then, she crumpled. Not to the ground, but into herself. Her shoulders began trembling. Her hands covered her mouth as tears welled and spilled down her flushed cheeks.

Midas panicked then. He stepped back in shame. His head lowered and his heart raced uncomfortably. *Did I hurt her? Did I say it wrong? Why does she cry?*

He opened his mouth to try and form any of the words he knew. *Safe. Me. Dragon.* None of them came out.

But Elowen surged forward, and to his complete astonishment, she touched him. She threw her frail arms around the curve of his neck and buried her face in his half-scaled flesh, sobbing softly.

Midas did not know what to do, so he froze. Every muscle locked into place, trying to understand. But then her warmth began to soak into him, and she did not move. She was so fragile. So soft. An ache bloomed from his chest as he felt her shake against him.

He did not know this strange gesture, but he knew it wasn't pain. She wasn't screaming, she wasn't running, she was *clinging* to him.

Midas shifted slightly, then awkwardly curled his new arms around her. *Like this?* he wondered. *Is this what I'm meant to do?*

She stayed like that in his arms, crying. He took a deep breath and tried a new word: "Elowen," he said. She pulled back to look at him. He repeated her name again, more confidently this time. She nodded, still crying.

"Yes. Yes, I'm Elowen," she said, giving him that soft smile he had come to adore. Her eyes roamed this new form of his. She did not look away from the horns or the wings or the tail. She did not flinch at the scales that decorated his body. Her fingers lifted, and she tenderly ran the tips over a patch of scales at his collarbone. The touch sent shivers down his spine.

"You're beautiful," she whispered, and Midas thought she might have been speaking to herself, so he did not answer.

She wrapped her arms around him again, resting her head on his chest. She held him like she had done before, and he returned it as carefully as he could, minding his claws.

His wings quivered behind him, and his tail curled around her ankles just to be closer. To be touched. To be known. To not be feared.

FIFTEEN

It wasn't just one gift anymore. It was many.

A silver comb, because he noticed the knots in her hair. A dark velvet cloak she now slept beneath only when she was with him, because he saw her shiver at the change of the seasons. The many stems of roses because he watched her touch the soft petals.

And food. *So much food* that even Elowen noticed her body began filling out, most noticeable in her face, where she looked less sallow and pale.

Elowen, though young, was not blind to the patterns or the intention. At first, she had believed the gifts were simply a gesture of returned kindness. But she knew now that they weren't thank-yous. They were offerings.

It felt silly when a thought crossed her mind, that Midas might have been courting her, but it felt that way less so when he had shifted into a form as close to a human as he could manage, just to say her name.

Weeks later, he was near the lake, lapping at the shallows of the water for a drink when she worked up the courage to ask about it.

"Midas?" she asked. He looked up immediately, golden eyes catching hers. "Can I ask you something?"

His head tilted in that strangely elegant way he had when he was curious and trying his best to understand her words. She stepped closer and sat at the lake's edge next to him.

"Why do you bring me so many things?"

He blinked slowly at her, then he rose to his full height and stepped away from her, a safer distance for him to shift. He hesitated, but finally, with a grunt of effort and a quiet whine of pain, he changed.

His human form stumbled forward, knees folding beneath him for a moment before he caught himself. His chest heaved, muscles trembling faintly under skin that shimmered with scale-patches and long streaks of gold.

His eyes hurt her, because he looked *nervous*. Not just uncertain—*vulnerable*. Like she might strike him where he stood. Or reject him. Or any number of horrible things he had endured at the hands of other humans.

"Gift," he said, voice rough from the change.

"I know," Elowen said softly, moving closer in the grass. "I know they are gifts. But...why so many? You bring me things every day now. And I—I think I understand what you're trying to say, but I want to hear it. If you know the words."

Midas swallowed. His gaze fell to the ground, tail curling around his side in a defensive coil. He looked like a boy who feared being scolded, not a mighty dragon.

Finally, he said: "For you. From me."

Her throat tightened. "They are beautiful, Midas. But…I can't take them home with me. You know that."

He gestured toward the forest, in the direction of her village. "Not home," he agreed. He thumped his chest proudly. "*Home.*"

Her eyes burned. He meant himself. His home. *His heart.* The gifts weren't just things. They were promises. They were symbols. They were the only way he knew how to express what he was trying to say to her.

She sat beside him, sliding her soft, gentle hand over his claws.

"I think I understand now," she whispered. Midas looked at her, brow furrowed, waiting. She smiled gently. "You're not just giving me gifts. You're asking me to belong. To stay. With you."

He nodded once, slow and solemn, then flipped his hand over to press their palms together, before lacing his fingers between hers.

They sat there quietly for a while. Elowen sighed as his warmth filled her bones. She shifted to rest her cheek against the hardened scales of his shoulder, but he winced slightly when he adjusted to fit her more comfortably at his side. He shook when he turned his neck or lifted his hands to brush the unruly hair away from his golden eyes. These transformations weighed on him—she could see it in the way his shoulders sagged and the trembling of his breath. His skin did not look thick and strong, it looked almost translucent in the light.

He was human-shaped, but not human, and this form hurt him. Elowen watched as he leaned forward a bit to look at his reflection on the surface of the lake. His face shimmered back at him from the water. Horns, wings, tail, golden eyes that had seen lifetimes. The dragon parts of him had not disappeared, they clung to him, lest he forget what he truly was.

But he had done this—endured this pain, changed his body—for her. He had approached her that day, shy and silent and afraid. She ran her free hand up his arm and turned his face to her with a gentle press to his cheek. His chest rose and fell faster under her gaze.

"You don't have to do this," she said softly. Her thumb stroked away a strand of dark hair and tucked it behind his ear. "You don't have to change yourself for me."

He blinked. A flicker of understanding passed across his face, but not the whole of it. He tilted his head, silently asking her to continue, so he could try better to listen.

Elowen tried again, slower. Simpler. He was not unintelligent, but he was learning, and she owed him that as a courtesy. "You are a dragon. I am not afraid of you. You do not have to hurt to be closer to me."

He carefully watched her lips as she spoke, furrowing his brows in concentration. He looked down where their fingers were still intertwined, then back up at her face before turning to look away, down to the water again, as if he was ashamed.

Perhaps he thought she was saying that she did not like this form–that she saw it as weakness. Or maybe he thought she did not see the beauty in it as he saw in her. Ache twisted in her heart at the thought that he truly cared about these things.

She gently turned his head the same way she did before, to meet his golden eyes again. She tried again, to communicate with him in a way he would understand. She pressed her palm into his hot chest, never moving her gaze from his, and quietly said: "Home."

She knew he understood by the way his back straightened with confidence. His tail wrapped around her, and his wing shielded her from a sudden gust of wind. He lifted his free hand to hers, lacing his fingers with hers as he did with the other.

And so there they stayed, a fierce creature of fire and gentle lady of the forest, until the sunset separated them once more.

SIXTEEN

THE MORTAR SLIPPED in Elowen's hand, the pestle clattering noisily against the stone bowl. Her father turned sharply at the sound, his lined face narrowing with quiet suspicion.

He had been watching her more closely these past few days, eyes catching details she had hoped would go unnoticed. She kept her head down, focusing on the withering leaves in her grasp. They crumbled too easily—brittle and useless like many of the things she had gathered recently.

"Elowen."

"Yes, father?" she asked, trying to sound unaffected.

"I took inventory of our stores."

Her stomach tightened. "Oh?"

"You've been returning with less. And yet..." His voice trailed off, eyes scanning her face, her arms, the slight curve returning to her hips, no longer sunken and sharp with hunger. "You look well-fed." Her fingers stilled. He stepped closer. "Have you been hiding ingredients?" he asked, voice quiet from wandering ears, but lacking in gentleness. "Keeping food for yourself?"

"No." The lie left her mouth too fast. He said nothing. Elowen took a breath, reaching for a safer half-truth. "It's the forest, father. The change in season. It's harder now to find what we need. I've tried, but—"

"You're lying." His voice hardened. "You walk into those woods every day and come back with barely enough to treat a cough, and yet you stand here, plumper than all the women in the town."

She looked down at her hands. "I'll do better."

His gaze turned sharper, the way it always did when he was about to say something that would leave a mark. "See that you do," he said. "Or I'll be forced to report it to the Council."

Her breath caught in her throat. "You would turn me in?"

He stepped away, the firelight dancing cruelly across the edges of his face. "I will not protect a traitor. And I will not be punished for your failings."

The words sliced. She stood frozen as he turned back to his workbench, the clink of glass vials and dried stems resuming with mechanical precision. Elowen's fingers dug into her skirts to keep them from trembling.

"I'll return tomorrow," she whispered, "with enough. I promise."

ELOWEN ARRIVED at the lake once more, breathless and fast, her eyes not searching for Midas, but scanning the under-brush with the sharpest eyes she'd had in weeks.

Midas rose slowly from his resting place behind the thick trees, careful not to startle her. The scent of her fear met him, sharp and bitter.

Something had frightened her. Something had hurt her.

She didn't look at him. Didn't speak. Didn't even acknowledge he was there. She dropped to her knees in the mossy soil, her fingers diving into the earth. She tugged at roots. She ripped herbs from their beds. She moved without grace now, only a strange urgency.

His chest rumbled, stepping closer and making a quiet rumbling sound. Still, she didn't turn to him.

Her satchel was open, half-filled with leaves and stems. She muttered under her breath words he didn't understand. Words he tried to hear, but they passed too fast, too soft.

His tail curled low behind him, uneasy, wondering if he had done something to upset her, for why else would she not look at him?

But he continued to listen to her. Her heartbeat was no longer slow and calm like before. It was frantic. Choked. She trembled when she leaned too far forward, catching herself on her hands. Her fingernails were dirt-caked and shaking. She looked pale with fright.

Midas looked toward the trees. The direction of her village. He growled, deep and resonant, and the forest shiv-ered with it.

Elowen flinched. She turned at last, eyes wide and wet. "No—no, please," she said quickly, crawling toward him on her knees, both hands raised. "Please don't be angry."

He stilled. She pressed a hand to his chest, right where his scales met his softer under-flesh. "I'm not afraid of them," she whispered, then wrapped her small arms around him as best she could. "I'm afraid they'll take this away."

Midas blinked. Slowly. He didn't understand, but she continued on.

"I've been careless. Coming back with less and less, just to spend time with you. My father noticed. He thinks I'm hiding ingredients. If I don't bring back enough, he'll tell the Council. They'll ban me from coming back."

Midas stiffened. *Ban her?* From *him?*

No. No, he could not allow that.

She let him go, and he leaned down, pressing his snout gently to the top of her head, breathing her scent of crushed herbs and salt-tears.

Then he moved past her, toward the edge of the trees, furious at the thought of anyone taking her away from him.

She ran to cut him off, small hands raised to stop him. "No. Midas. Please...don't go." He looked at her, and her voice trembled. "I just need to fix it. I can't lose this. I can't lose *you.*"

The ache that bloomed in his chest was new. Unfamiliar. He lowered himself back down beside her, folding his wings inward as he watched her hands return to the earth, gentler now, but still desperate.

After a while, when her satchel was nearly full and her breathing had calmed, she sat beside him on the mossy bank and whispered, "You have to stop feeding me."

Midas stilled once again. His golden eyes blinked slowly. She looked up at him, guilt on her face. "My father has noticed that I'm looking stronger. Healthier. It's *wrong* to them. Suspicious. They think I'm stealing food. They'll blame me for the missing goat."

Blame her? Blame her for what Midas had done?

Her voice broke, and she dropped her gaze to her lap. "I don't want to go hungry, but I will if it means I can still see you. So...no more food. Please."

For a moment, there was only silence. And then the forest *shook*. Midas' wings flared wide behind him, striking branches. His tail lashed the earth, gouging the soil. A thunderous *growl* rolled from his throat—furious and *wounded*.

Elowen shrank back, startled. His outburst disturbed all the creatures of the forest and all of the trees.

"Shhhh, shhhh, please!" she begged, afraid someone might hear him. "This is the only way—" Midas growled, not at her, but enough that she understood that he was refusing her. "Midas—"

He pressed his snout to her head and growled again, breath hot and ragged with anger. But not directed at her. *Never* directed at her.

Elowen's hands came up slowly to rub along the scales lining his jaw, calming him. Her eyes were brimming with tears. "Okay. Everything will be okay."

Midas huffed, smoke curling from his nose. It was not the answer he wanted to hear, but he also knew that he did not like seeing her this way.

He knew he could not force Elowen to leave that cruel village, however much he could see them killing her slowly.

SEVENTEEN

ELOWEN HAD DONE what she promised, and for five days, she made sure to bring as much as her satchel could carry with her back to the village. Her father did not question her again, and he did not need to.

They did not give second chances here—not even to their own family.

Elowen had slept in later than usual. Her body had grown weak again, as she forced herself to vomit up what Midas fed her every day after they parted. She tried to lose weight, to throw off any suspicious eyes and it made her tired and lethargic.

She was helping her father make a batch of rash salve when the shouting started.

The two of them stood in the doorway of their home as a man stormed through the village square. His eyes were wild, breath frantic with each word.

"I saw it!" he yelled. "High above the cliffs just this day

before the morn! Wings the size of rooftops, black as night, cloaked in smoke and ash and fire! Dragon! Dragon!"

People spilled from their homes, muttering, scoffing, gasping. Some crossed their arms in disbelief, others looked to the skies in fear.

The man pointed toward the mountains. "It's the beast that has been stealing our livestock! The goats! The chickens! The cows! It will starve us all!"

"Drunk," Elowen's neighbor said.

Her father nodded in agreement. "A coward stirring up trouble."

Elowen didn't speak, she was frozen in place. Her stomach turned. *Someone had spotted Midas.*

The Council arrived soon after, cloaks stiff and masks glowing a bright ivory in the sun. The Council did not tolerate lies, but they did honor the old ways, and if there was a dragon, Elowen knew they would deal with it in the same way their ancestors did.

Midas was in danger.

Elowen tried to sneak away, to warn him that he had been spotted, but one of the Councilmen pointed a crooked finger at her.

"You there! Forest girl! Speak quickly, have you seen any signs of this beast in the forest?"

Elowen's face was tense, and she slowly shook her head. They believed her, of course. What sane woman would see a dragon and keep quiet about it?

They turned to the man once more, listening to his description of the dragon. Elowen knew he wasn't lying to them, because he described Midas too accurately.

And then, as always, the Council acted.

"If a dragon remains," one started, "it must be destroyed."

Another added: "If it has already stolen from our fields, then it will not stop at livestock."

They all agreed with each other, quietly discussing amongst themselves for a moment, before turning to Elowen's father.

"We must lure it," they said. "Healer, we require poison."

Elowen's throat tightened. Her father nodded obediently. "What kind?"

"A salve as potent as you can manage, enough to weaken the beast if not kill it, so we may finish the job by our own hands." His eyes flicked to Elowen's from under his mask. "You will help," he commanded.

She said nothing, and quietly followed her father back into their home. He dug through dusty shelves for a while, pulling out an old tome Elowen had never seen him reference before. Her father opened it carefully, flipping through the stiff pages until he found what he was looking for. He straightened his broken glasses on the tip of his nose and fingered down the page as he read.

Without looking up, he began reading off ingredients, expecting Elowen to gather them. "Iron Ivyleaf. Widow's tongue. Ashenshroom. Sap of Blackbark." He looked up for a moment, scowling at her as she stood unmoving. "With haste, girl, we don't have much time."

He continued reading down the page of all the most toxic and deadly ingredients in their world. His words did not tremble, but every movement in Elowen's body did.

She crushed the herbs, ground the roots, mixed the

oils with the powders into a thick, muddy-colored salve that stung the hairs in her nostrils and made her eyes water.

When they were done, her father gathered the large bowl and had her follow him back out into the square where a sacrificial goat waited. It was tied to the whipping post, its eyes too large for its skull.

Elowen shook as her and her father dipped their hands into the bowl. They rubbed the salve across the goat's hide, steady and even, coating its flank, its shoulder, its spine. No one spoke, but she knew they were being carefully watched by the Council.

Once it was coated in the poison, they demanded her and her father lead the goat to the tree line to let it free. She watched, trying her best to hide her tears as the forest swallowed it whole.

What had she done?

The scent of poison clung to her, and it made her sick. She was under the eyes of her father and the Council, and so no matter how badly she wanted to, she could not rush into the forest to warn Midas. Not yet, at least.

When the sun went down, she would sneak out, to find him. It was a long few hours for her, filled with anxiety and guilt unlike anything she had felt before. Her heart hammered in her ears, her skin itched, and her eyes remained wet with tears.

When she finally heard her father begin to snore, Elowen quietly snuck out of her little cottage. She could not leave through the front gates like normal, for the guards were keeping careful watch for the dragon. She had to climb up the rough stone wall and crawl over the top. It was dark, and her body was weak with hunger, but she forced herself to climb.

She had to let instinct bring her to the lake, for it was too dark to see and in her haste she had not thought to bring a torch or candle with her.

The forest was colder at night, and she tripped over branches she'd normally float over. She felt like she was being watched, but not in the protective kind way she felt when Midas was hiding in the trees. No. She felt threatened.

Her heart was lodged in her throat by the time she made it to the lake, barely lit by the crescent moon. It shimmered faintly beneath the cloudy sky.

The moment she stepped into the clearing, she loudly called out for Midas. There was no response. She called out again. Everything was so still, even the trees.

Then, finally, in the dimmest of light, she caught the glimmer of his gold-kissed scales. She let out a sigh of relief as she saw Midas looking down at the goat, still alive, not yet consumed.

"Midas!" she shouted. As she approached, he lifted his attention from the goat, and a low rumble left his throat that shook the trees. She could see it in his eyes, he was angry.

Elowen raised her shaking hands. "Please listen."

His nostrils flared, and he inhaled deeply.

The moment he caught her scent and the poison lingering on it, the sound that left his throat was not a growl, it was a roar. It made the ground tremble, sent the gentle water of the lake rippling, and nearly made her lose her footing.

"Midas!" she cried. "Please, it's not what you think!"

But he was already baring his teeth, and smoke began to build as the rage in his throat came alight.

You smell of this poison, he said in his language, though he knew she could not hear it. *Do you take me for a fool?!*

Elowen's eyes filled with tears. "I had no choice. But I came to warn you, please understand—"

Lies, he roared back, and then he snapped his jaws, barely missing her legs. The sound was like thunder, and Elowen screamed with a fear she's never known. *Humans. Always. Lie.*

Elowen tried to take a step forward. "I would never hurt you."

He recoiled from her, wings flaring wide, the fire in his throat making the air around him glow orange. *Go away!* he shouted.

"Please believe me," she begged, pressing her hands to her chest, her heart aching from a pain she's never known.

He lunged forward again. He got close enough that the razor-sharp edge of his teeth caught the hem of her dress, tearing off a piece of the cloth. *Go!*

Though Elowen could not understand his words, she felt it in his actions. He did not want her there. He did not trust her anymore. She sobbed, ragged and helpless as she backed away. "I'm sorry," she whispered. "I'm so sorry, Midas."

For a heartbeat, she thought he might stop her, but he just growled again, orange light leaking from his mouth. Her tears fell freely as she walked lifelessly back to her village.

Her cries were so loud that she did not notice the movement in the woods around her. She did not notice the whispers.

Somewhere, deep in the woods, near the lake where they had met, Midas lowered his head, trembling with rage and grief.

The scent of her was still clinging to his nostrils, sweet, familiar, but beneath it all...

Poison. Betrayal.

Midas was no fool. He smelled the salve long before he saw the goat. He knew the humans had sent it to kill him, but he was too old, too strong for such weak poison to do much more than make him salivate sickly. He had intended to kill the goat and leave its carcass far away from the lake so that it did not poison the water Elowen drank.

But when she emerged, and he smelled that same poison on her, he had never felt as destroyed as he did in that moment. He trusted her. He...*cared* for her. How could she do such a thing?

Midas stayed there near the lake, pacing in circles. He had half a mind to scorch her village for her treachery, to be rid of them entirely.

But he could hear her crying as she returned home. It was not a cry of deceit, it was real, from deep in her chest, as if she truly had lost something when he sent her away. It twisted something painful inside of him.

Then after a while, he heard something in the distance.

He raised his head sharply, golden eyes narrowing toward the east. The direction of her village. The air trembled faintly, carrying faint vibrations to his ears: shouts, muffled screams, and then—

Crack.

It was not thunder. Not lightning. No natural sound he had ever heard. He heard it again. Again. And again.

Midas' heart stuttered. His claws sank into the soil, curling until the ground split beneath them. He strained his senses, forcing his body to still, to *listen*.

Then, he heard a cry, high and raw and human.

Elowen!

EIGHTEEN

SHE SAW the torches before she reached the gate.

And the men holding them.

Two guards stood just outside the village wall, faces pale in the firelight, swords drawn. Next to them, stood the man who had been shouting of dragons, and even more painfully, her father.

Her blood ran cold.

The guards began to bark at her. "By order of the Council, you are to be seized and brought forth for punishment."

She didn't run, didn't beg. She should have known someone would have noticed her sneak away, but she hadn't expected her own father to turn her in, however much he might have threatened it before.

Elowen let her hands fall slowly to her sides, and nodded once. They bound her wrists with rough rope and marched her through the gates and into the center of the town.

The entire village had gathered beneath the cold sky,

stormclouds rolling in heavy and fast. The downpour was loud, but not as loud as the Council loudly proclaimed her a traitor.

They didn't ask her to explain, nor did they offer a trial. Their bone-carved masks flashed with the lightning above their heads.

"Twenty lashes. No less. We must purge the treason from her blood!"

The punishment post stood tall in the center of the square, a wooden beam stained with blood, time, and pain. Elowen's legs trembled as they tied her to the post, and she whimpered as they forced her to her knees. She began to cry when they cut open the back of her dress, not because of her immodesty, but because she knew the pain would come next.

The wind and rain bit against her bare skin as the storm howled with its own harsh judgement.

The whip cracked through the silence, ripping across her back like fire. She screamed, but the second one was worse. By the third, she could hardly breathe. By the fourth, she was begging for mercy—mercy she knew no one would give.

They didn't stop. By the tenth, she was barely conscious, delirious from the pain, crying because it was only half over. She began to wonder if she would even make it that long. Her voice had gone hoarse, and her breath came in ragged, uneven gasps. What remained of her dress was heavy with her blood and the rain.

She felt the world go quiet, and Elowen thought she had finally died. She looked up as lightning cracked across the sky overhead, painting the world in a flash of white for naught but a second.

And in that flash, she saw a shadow. Massive, unmoving, perched atop the stone wall of her village. Another bolt lit the world again, and the shape became more clear.

"Midas..." Elowen croaked, her voice nothing against the wind and the rain and the thunder.

He stepped closer, descending from the wall like a god of legends, rain falling off him in waves. His golden eyes burned through the downpour, and his breath grew orange against the cold and the dark.

He did not roar, he did not run, he walked deliberately, silently toward her, every step shaking the very stones beneath her knees. He stopped in front of her, his eyes scanning her small, broken, bloody form. He saw the way she was tied to the post, and then his eyes landed on the man in a mask made of dragon bone, holding a whip.

And Midas snarled. It wasn't a roar, it was darker, lower. It was far more terrifying than anything she'd ever heard. It was not a warning, it was harsher than that.

He lunged forward, his teeth biting the man holding the whip in half. He did not eat the body, he left both parts there in the square for the others to see. Then, he raised his sharp claws and slashed clean through the ropes tying Elowen to the post.

She collapsed forward, and he caught her gently with his claws. He curled the talons around her with a tenderness he'd never shown anything before. He lifted her away from the cruel village, and carried her into the storm.

Sʜᴇ ʜᴀᴅ ʙᴇᴇɴ ᴛᴇʟʟɪɴɢ the truth.

Though she smelled of the poison, she had come to warn him. She risked everything for him.

And he had *growled* at her. Driven her away. Called her a liar. Doubted her, doubted everything they had built together in the serenity of that forest.

Her body hung limp in his claws, breathing shallow, as he carried her into the mountains, into the very depths of his cave, where he could shield her from the cruel village that would bleed her dry for her kindness.

He would never forgive himself for making her bleed. He might as well have held the whip himself.

Midas set Elowen down gently in a pile of coins, for he had nothing softer for her. Her back was a ruin of flesh— long red welts that bled from the ripped skin.

Midas didn't know what to do. She lay broken there because of him, wheezing in pain. He lowered his great head near her back, and even his breath fanning across her bare back made her flinch violently.

A sound rose in his chest. A sound of grief—wild and terrible. Hesitantly, his tongue flicked out and he began to lick the wounds. He was soft and careful, like a lion grooming her cubs. It was instinct. It was an apology. It was a promise that he would never doubt her again.

She whimpered. Midas stilled. He watched her soft,

slender fingers twitch and moved to meet her eyes, half-opened and leaking tears.

"Midas," she cried softly. He pressed his snout gently into her fingers. He made a soft sound of sorry, and her mouth twitched into a joyless smile. "Thank you."

Then, she slipped into sleep once more.

And Midas, ancient and mighty and ferocious, curled around her like a fortress of scales and fire. He thought of that village once more, and his body tensed with rage. If Elowen had not been in such a state, he would have stayed and razed it to the ground.

They had tied those same gentle hands that mended their wounds and healed their illnesses to a post and struck her until her blood pooled on the stones.

He had scorched villages for less.

She does not belong to them anymore, he thought. *She is mine now.*

But not as a treasure. She was not his to be locked away or hoarded or hidden. She was his like fire was his.

Midas ached to groom her wounds again, but did not want to wake her to pain. *No*, he had to learn softness. He had to learn tenderness.

He had to learn all the things he almost lost when he forced her away.

NINETEEN

Elowen woke to warmth at her back. It wasn't the heat of fire, though one cracked softly nearby in a crater carved into the stone. It also wasn't the burn of the lashes down her back, for that was aching and wrong. This warmth was... different. Soothing, almost like being held in a dream and gently coaxed awake.

She blinked slowly to the sight of moss above her head and the smell of earth surrounding her. And...something else sharp and wild.

She shifted and winced, her body shivering with white-hot pain. She trembled as she moved, and her body broke into a new sweat as her skin pulled tight at her back. The simple act of breathing made the pain worse.

But she was alive, and somehow, she remembered why.

The pain had stolen her cries for mercy, and yet, Midas had still come for her. She remembered the flash of him in the lightning, the way the world went quiet at his approach.

She turned her head, just slightly, and he was there.

He wasn't sleeping of course. He never truly rested where she was involved. He was coiled around her like a living barricade, one of his wings hovering above her to block out the light from the fire in case it was too bright for her tired eyes. His body radiated heat, and his breath was slow and controlled as his golden eyes watched her.

Her lips cracked painfully when she tried to force a smile. He dipped his head at once, the tip of his snout gently nudging her hairline. He inhaled, checking for the stench of sickness, of infection.

"Midas," she whispered to him, just so that he knew she saw him, that she still trusted him, and that she felt safe there wrapped in his tail. He rumbled back to her, quietly, answering in his own way.

Her lips smacked together, dry and crusty. Midas nudged a shallow clay bowl closer to her mouth with his claw, and even slightly tilted it so that she wouldn't have to strain to take a drink.

With the burn in her throat cooled by the water, her eyes met his again. "I'm sorry," she murmured. "I tried to warn you. I would never hurt you, Midas." Her throat closed as tears pricked in her eyes once more. "They forced me to make the poison."

His chest rumbled again, and he simply offered her more water, staying there unmoving until she finished the bowl. His way of showing that he believed her.

With the help of his tail, he propped her up slightly, and that's when she got her first real look at where they were. It was a large, cool cave, every inch of the walls piled high with golden coins and other treasures. In the corner nearest the fire, there was a small pile of what she could only describe as *human things*: dried meats, a basket of fruits, jars of creams that smelled of potent healing salves, water, and even a pile of clothes, pelts, and blankets. Not things a dragon would make space for, but things he had gathered for her.

Elowen suddenly began to sob into his scales, hiccuping thank yous in between breaths. Midas simply tightened his tail coiled around her, careful not to shift her too much or too quickly.

She drifted in and out of sleep after that for a few more hours. When she would wake, Midas would always have another bowl of water ready. Once, she stirred awake to find a perfectly ripe pear, crushed by his claws so that she didn't have to force her teeth through the skin.

And all the time, she clung to him like she was afraid it was all a dream.

It had been six days since Midas brought Elowen to his cave.

Outside, the world moved on, but in the cave, time was slow. Life thinned itself down to the barest essentials: warmth, breath, water, pain, rest, healing.

Midas had not left the cave once.

He had no need to, of course. He had been gathering things for her for weeks now—slowly trying to work up the courage to show her that she had a place amongst his hoard. But suddenly, that hoard held no pull, not when the most precious treasure he had ever known was an injured, fragile thing nestled in the coil of his tail.

He watched her sleep for hours. Not in a possessive way as he guarded his treasures, but in a vigilant way, for he would not let the cruelty of the world touch her again.

Now, when she woke, she smiled at him. Always smiling. And his tail, scaled and heavy, always moved with her. It was safer than interacting with her with his wings or his claws, for his tail possessed more fine dexterity than the rest of him. It was his way of shielding her.

He could not say it in her language yet, but Elowen could see it in his actions. Moreso, she saw it in an alcove carved into the cave walls, where the little treasures Midas had shared with her sat like a shrine. The pretty stone, a fresh rose, one of his scales, and even the dried flower crown she had made for him.

Elowen reached out, her hand trembling with emotion as she brushed her fingers along the delicate dried blooms tinged brown from age.

Midas watched quietly, his liquid gold eyes softening with her gentle presence alone. Her fingers left the flower crown to touch the sensitive patch of flesh just under his eye.

He leaned into her touch, and rumbled to her all the things he wanted to say to her, but did not have the human words for yet.

TWENTY

It had been three days since Elowen last spoke of what the village did to her.

Midas had felt the weight of it in his chest. He had not asked her to talk about it, but when she cried quietly in her sleep when she thought he could not hear, he'd simply curled his tail around her more tightly.

She did not once ask to leave, but neither did she choose to stay. He had brought her here for safety, for protection, but her silence made it hard for Midas to understand what more she needed. What more he could do to convince her to stay with him.

Now, as the moon hung high over the lake outside the cave, Midas sat alone beside the fire, his body folded into a shape that could almost pass as human. His horns casted sharp shadows across the stone, his long tail coiled neatly beside him.

Elowen slept nearby, her back rising and falling in steady rhythm, her face soft in the firelight.

He'd protected her. That much he knew. He'd broken her bonds. He'd carried her through the storm and licked her wounds clean with the only tenderness his body understood. He had brought her safety where others would bring her harm.

But was that care, or was it ownership? Dragons did not ask to keep things, and they *certainly* did not ask humans to *stay*.

But Elowen was more than gold or gems to be hidden in a cave. She was not prey or prize or offering. She had chosen to save him when no one else would, and he had mistakenly pushed her away for it. He had no reason to assume she would forgive him for that. She had whispered gratitudes to him many times for saving her, but Midas knew that in the human tongue, thankfulness and forgiveness were not the same thing.

Earlier that day, she had gathered some of the things he'd collected for her and organized them in a basket near the fire. He had felt the cold edge of panic then, afraid she would leave.

But he did not stop her, nor did he ask her to stay, because if she wanted to leave and he tried to stop her, she would never come back.

And that fate would be worse than losing her to the village.

Midas rose slowly and crossed closer to her sleeping form where he knelt beside her. He inhaled her scent like the first breath of summer. Carefully, with the very tip of his tail, he reached for her and brushed a single strand of hair away from her face.

"Stay," he begged quietly in human words. She stirred,

but she didn't wake. Instead, her hands shifted in her sleep and found the curve of his tail near her. She hugged it to her chest and exhaled with a deep breath of serenity.

Midas thought it was the most beautiful sight he had ever seen, for it was the first time he had ever been trusted.

Chosen.

He closed his eyes, whispering to her again three of his favorite words:

"Stay. Elowen. Safe."

ELOWEN AWOKE SLOWLY, the fire casting its warm glow across the stone walls of the cave. She blinked against the dimness, the flicker of firelight soft against her vision. Midas wasn't far. She could hear the low rumble of his breathing—the slow, steady sound of safety. She shifted slightly and turned her head.

He was curled nearby, not quite asleep. His eyes glowed faintly in the dark, slitted gold set deep into the contours of his not-quite-human face. She wondered how long he'd been watching her.

"Elowen." His voice was gravel and smoke. Not quite right, but trying. "You...hurt?"

She blinked at him, and shook her head. "No. I'm not hurting."

Midas tilted his head slightly. His gaze drifted toward her back, and she followed it instinctively, her breath catching at the memory. The post. The whip. The silence of the crowd. Her father.

Tears burned behind her eyes, but she refused to let them fall.

"Hurt," Midas repeated, though this time it was not poised as a question. It was a statement of fact. To him, her tears meant she was hurting, and she was, but not in the way he likely assumed.

Elowen shook her head again. She closed the distance between them, her knees resting on his thighs as she faced him. "No. I'm not hurting. I'm…sad."

Midas made a sound then, somewhere between a growl and a sigh. It wasn't of anger—it felt deeper than that. His tail curved around her again like it often did, never trapping, but shielding. Protecting.

He lifted his hand to her face, mindful of the claws at the ends of his fingers as he twisted a strand of her loose hair around them. He was careful not to yank it, but he wanted to compare it to his own that he mirrored after hers. His was thicker, darker, and lacked the elegant shine of hers.

"Midas," Elowen whispered again after a long silence. "I do not want to go back."

Her words made his breath catch, and he sat a little straighter as he met her gaze once more, golden eyes searching her lake-colored ones. "Stay," he said. "Safe."

She nodded. "Yes. I'd like to stay."

Midas exhaled slowly and lowered his head until he could nuzzle his human-like nose against her throat. It was a dragon's gesture, Elowen had learned. It meant trust.

She pressed her hands to his cheeks, holding his face in her palms. "You are safe with me, too."

His tail wrapped around her just a bit tighter, like a treasure he would never lose again. Now, she was no longer a guest in his cave.

She was his. And she was *home*.

TWENTY-ONE

When Elowen woke, there was a weight at her side. She cracked her eyes open, and Midas was there, curled around her with his wings outstretched like a canopy over her head.

He was already awake, watching her in his human form.

"Good morning," she rasped with a stretch, still quietly wincing at the tight, healing skin on her back. The worst of the burn had faded, but the throb was still persistent.

The cave smelled faintly of smoke and meat. She looked to the cooking pot perched over the firewood, and she heard the bubbling of a simple broth Midas had heated himself.

"You take better care of me than I deserve," she murmured, moving to the fire to smell the broth. She added a twig of rosemary and a pinch of coarse salt, stirring it gently as she brushed sleep from her eyes.

Midas tilted his head. "Deserve?" he asked from behind her.

Elowen smiled over her shoulder. "It means...that I've

done nothing to earn your kindness. That you take care of me despite what I am."

His brow furrowed. "Earn," he repeated. Then, he repeated it again, as if the word offended him. "You are Elowen. You deserve."

Something bloomed in her chest, but she said nothing back. He rose slowly, his limbs unfolding with that wild grace of the dragons. The scales peppering his human form shimmered slightly in the firelight, surrounding him in a halo of gold. He crouched next to her at the fire and inhaled the broth she was stirring.

He did this often, when she cooked, as if he was trying to discern exactly what she put into it to bring it to her liking. Midas was always learning. He dipped one of his claws into the broth and tasted it.

He made a strange face, and Elowen quietly giggled.

"Needs meat," he told her.

Elowen nodded. "You're right. I will add it soon, along with the carrots. Then it will be soup, not just broth."

He nodded, and continued to watch her work. There was something beautifully soft in the way he fussed over her. As she watched him watching her, she noticed his hands kept touching his face to brush away his long hair. It was irritating him, how it fell into his eyes, caught on his teeth, and pulled when he touched it.

Elowen grabbed his hands and lowered them for him. "Let me," she said, waiting for his permission. He cowered slightly, as if afraid of what she might do, but nodded slowly.

She carefully ran her fingers through a thick section of

his hair at the side of his head and began to braid it against his skull until it fell down his back.

When she finished braiding it, she went back to her soup as if it was nothing, a passing moment in her life that she'd forget in a few hours.

But for Midas, it meant so much more than that. She had sensed his discomfort with his hair, and more than that, she *relieved* that discomfort.

Midas swallowed the lump in his throat and nodded toward the soup she was now ladling into a bowl. "Eat," he commanded.

"Would you like some?" she asked, holding out the bowl for him. He made another face, and she laughed again before blowing on the broth softly. She pressed her lips to the bowl and took a sip of the hot liquid.

She sighed when the tension in her back seemed to melt away with the taste. They did not speak again while she ate, there was no need. Eventually, when the bowl was empty, Midas took it from her and set it to the side before handing her another filled with freshwater from a basin.

She sat cross-legged near the fire as she sipped from the bowl, and he had a passing thought that he should find her something of higher quality than clay—but the thought came and went from the forefront of his mind, replaced by the distraction that was her own hair.

He stared at it—the way it spilled down her back and over her shoulders in strands the color of rich bark.

Her hair had admittedly always fascinated him. It was so fine, so delicate, and so very pretty. His hand gently toyed with the end of the braid she had given him, and decided that he wanted to try giving her one.

He had seen her do it before, the way her fingers moved in a strange pattern and weaved the sections together. He had seen her do it so many times that surely he could master the action himself.

He leaned forward a bit and reached slowly for the ends of her hair. She turned slightly and hummed with curiosity. He froze, unsure and slightly embarrassed, but then he pinched some of her hair and pointed to the braid she had given him.

Elowen blinked, and then another light laugh slipped from her lips. "You want to try braiding my hair?"

He nodded, ears turning warm under her gaze in this *ridiculous* humanoid form. These ridiculous hands he had, useless for defense or flying, but perhaps gentle enough for this.

"Alright," she encouraged gently, shifting to sit in between his spread legs. Midas' back was straight as he reached out again as carefully as he could manage.

The strands of her hair slid all across his fingers like liquid, so hard to hold. He separated it all into three clumsy bundles, and squinted in concentration. He stared at the hair in his hands for a long time before realizing he hadn't paid enough attention to her braiding at all.

His first attempt wasn't even a weave so much as a knot. He huffed, and Elowen stifled a laugh.

"Not as easy as it looks?" she asked him.

He let out a grumble from low in his throat at her teasing, and tried again. This time, he managed three passes before the strands slipped from his fingers once more.

No matter how many times he made a mess of it, she simply shook out the knots for him and let him try again and again. Eventually, with careful patience and grumbles under his breath, he presented her with a lopsided, uneven plait of hair that vaguely resembled a braid.

She smiled as her hands felt over it, and looked up at him like he had just presented her with the finest gem. "Look at this," she said, leaning forward slightly after turning to face him. "My ferocious dragon braided my hair."

Midas huffed, tail thumping against the cave floor in feigned annoyance, but something in his chest felt warm and sated.

Her fingers brushed over his awkward hand, and she leaned into his chest. "Thank you."

He looked down at her, so small, showing him this... foreign affection. It felt wrong, but it also felt right.

He was learning her still—always learning. And thus far, he had learned to be gentle in a way he never saw the humans be.

Let alone the dragons.

TWENTY-TWO

Elowen no longer winced when she bent forward. Her back still ached, in the way half-healed wounds always did— tight and tender. The worst of the pain had passed. The bruises had faded too, replaced by raised pink skin mapping out the scars to come.

She moved carefully as she swept the dust from the stone floor with a bundle of dried herbs, the scent of them meeting her as she worked.

Midas watched her from the shadowed curve of the cavern wall, one wing tucked tightly to his side, the other stretched lazily behind him. His eyes tracked every motion —each twist of her waist, each soft breath of exertion. He said nothing, but she felt his gaze like sunlight against her skin.

"Don't worry," she said over her shoulder. "I'm being careful."

He grunted softly, the sound somewhere between a chuff and a sigh. She didn't take offense. She'd learned, by now, that Midas communicated in subtle ways. The twitch of his tail when she stood up with a wince. The way he always positioned himself between her and the entrance to the cave. The way he gathered fresh food for her and left it near the fire so she wouldn't have to forage herself.

Or how, when she cried in her sleep, she always woke up curled into his warmth.

Elowen reached into a basket near her makeshift bed and withdrew several pieces of polished metal and broken jewelry—trinkets from Midas' hoard that she had carefully chosen over the last few days. One by one, she began arranging them along the stone shelf near the cave wall. A golden chalice with ivy designs. A silver comb. A cracked hand mirror.

Dragons didn't share. She knew that. This was *his* sanctuary and *his* hoard. But Midas...he let her touch them, and gave no growl or warning when she did. No possessive snarl that indicated it bothered him.

He simply watched as though he had been gathering it all for her in the first place. Maybe, in some fated way, he did, and that's why it never bothered him when she dug through the piles of treasures.

Elowen's presence in his cave shifted the air in ways Midas hadn't foreseen. Her scent lingered on everything, so much so he wondered if it had soaked into his very own scales like rain into soil.

He didn't mind it, he just didn't know what to do with it.

She moved among his hoard like she had always belonged there. She hummed under her breath as she turned old trinkets into decorations.

And Midas, the giant, ancient thing that he was, stood frozen against the walls of the cave, terrified she might leave if he so much as breathed wrong.

His tail absently thumped against the cave ground, disturbing a pile of coins. They clattered to the ground noisily, pulling Elowen's attention in his direction.

She stepped forward, unafraid, and looked at the pile near his tail and his stance against the cave wall.

"I can stop," she said softly, "If I'm upsetting you."

He wanted to say *No. Never.* That she could keep every bauble. That she could *have* the cave if it meant she stayed. But words were impossible in this form, and so instead he lowered his massive head and bowed it until he could touch her shoulder with the end of his snout.

She smiled at him. A warm, human smile that made his entire chest ache with yearning for something with her he could not yet name.

She reached out to touch his snout, and Midas, the old foolish beast that he was, trusted her enough to lean into it.

Midas had left earlier that day, flying off into the mist-heavy morning. Elowen hadn't asked where he was going, she never did, because she knew he'd come back before nightfall. She didn't want him to stay curled up in the cave with her all the time anyway, for a creature as large and majestic as him deserved to kiss the skies the way she wished she could.

In his absence, she moved through the cavern. The piles of gold and trinkets glittered like autumn light, and though she never took anything, she'd begun to tidy them to give herself something to do. And partially, to uncover the stories that might still linger beneath centuries of dust and loss.

Near the far back wall, beneath a pile of silver goblets, she found a cloth.

She blinked and knelt, brushing the edge with her fingers. The fabric was faded and worn, dulled by time, but still soft to the touch. Carefully, she dragged it out, coughing softly as a cloud of dust billowed upward.

It was a tapestry.

Not grand or particularly ornate, but still detailed. The embroidery was old, done with skillful hands and slow stitches. Elowen laid it flat on the stone floor, her breath catching in her throat.

Dragons.

Dozens of them, stretching their wings across the weave in a pride of crimson, silver, storm-gray, gold. Her fingers hovered over the central dragon.

It was golden. Massive. Regal. And at its side, nestled beneath one outstretched wing, was a smaller dragon with a darker hue. A hatchling.

But where the others were bright with color, this small one had worn thin. The thread had faded, the image of the hatchling nearly invisible now, its body rubbed raw from touch.

Elowen felt her heart tighten.

She wasn't certain how she knew but this tapestry had once brought Midas comfort. He had come to it again and again. Not for the strength of dragons or the pride of flight.

But for the memory of his mother.

Her gaze blurred as tears welled in her eyes. Elowen sat back on her heels and gently gathered the edges of the tapestry in her lap. She stroked the corner of the fabric where the faded hatchling lay and whispered, "I'm so sorry you were alone for so long."

A sound behind her stirred the air. She didn't turn. She didn't need to.

She felt Midas—sensed his presence filling the cave with heat and weight and breath. A low huff escaped him, and Elowen turned to face him, still holding the tapestry in her lap. His eyes glowed faintly in the firelight, watching. Silent.

"My mother died when I was young, too," she admitted, her voice fragile but steady. "She was sweet. Too sweet for our village. She loved music. Dancing. Things that weren't allowed."

She swallowed, brushing her thumb along the edge of the tapestry. "She went out to pick wildflowers for our shop, but made the mistake of keeping a butter-yellow one for herself on her nightstand. The Council said that was against the law. She was lashed until she got an infection, and then she died of fever."

Midas' breath caught—a low, rasping sound in his throat.

Elowen looked down at the tapestry again. Smoothed the image of the dragons. Carefully, she stood and moved toward a small niche in the stone wall she'd cleared earlier. She folded the tapestry with trembling hands, then placed the bundle inside the alcove and stepped back, brushing a strand of hair from her face.

"There," she whispered. "Now she won't be lost again."

When she turned, Midas was still watching her. Something deep in his eyes shifted, like she had uncovered a most beloved memory from the very depths of his heart.

He moved toward her slowly, tail dragging behind him like a chain. He lowered his head to the alcove and breathed in deep, letting the scent of the tapestry and her hands settle in his lungs.

Then he looked at her, leaned in, and gently pressed his forehead to hers. And in the silence, she felt him say *thank you.*

TWENTY-THREE

Elowen sat cross-legged near the hearth, her hair unbound, a blanket wrapped around her shoulders. Across from her, Midas knelt in his human form, his wings curled close, tail resting still against the floor. His chest was exposed, the firelight painting golden warmth across the scales that scattered like constellation fragments over his collarbone and shoulders. His long dark hair fell forward, shadowing his brow as he concentrated.

A deep breath. His tongue pressed awkwardly against the words he had spent hours rehearsing. He had been practicing the human tongue often lately, and had begun to grasp it enough to form full sentences, however simple they may be.

"I...want...to tell you," he said, slow and careful. "About my things."

Elowen tilted her head, encouraging. "Your treasures?"

He nodded once, pleased, she understood. "For practice."

Her smile was soft. "I'd love to hear about them."

His fingers twitched where they rested on his knee. He opened his mouth, then closed it again. He did not speak of the battles. Of the blood-soaked fields or the taste of ash. Not of the other dragons, not yet. Not of the humans with their spears and their fear.

He pointed instead to a flute that looked to be made of bone resting in a pile near her shoulder.

"That," he said, "was music. From the desert, far away. Wind will play it when no one touch."

Elowen turned to look at it, eyes wide. "What does it sound like?"

He thought about it for a while, trying to find the words. "Like..." He struggled for the word, frowned, then he pointed to her throat. "Like when you hum."

Elowen flushed. She lowered her gaze, her smile growing quiet. Midas cocked his head and nodded toward a polished necklace with an emerald near her hand. "Pretty like Elowen."

She let out a faint laugh. "You are very kind."

His tail shifted. His claws—duller in this form—curled softly against the floor. He didn't know the words to tell her how much she meant. How much she had changed him. Instead, he reached into a basket he had carried back in his teeth earlier, and pulled something small from it. It was a small plate painted to resemble the mountain and then glazed over to keep it pristine and shiny.

Elowen accepted it with both hands, examining the artwork. "It's beautiful."

Midas tilted his head, eyes bright with firelight. "You are...my mountain."

She looked up sharply, her flush growing deeper.

His cheeks felt warm too. "I mean…I feel…" He pressed a fist to his chest. "Safe. Safe with Elowen."

Her breath hitched. "I'm glad you feel safe with me. You make me feel safe too."

They sat in silence for a while. Not an awkward one, but the kind built from familiarity, from coexisting rhythms. From understanding that not everything needed words. Finally, Midas shifted forward and placed a gentle hand over hers.

"One day," he said slowly, "I tell you about dragons. Before the humans"

She nodded, wrapping her fingers around his. "And I'll listen when you're ready."

After a while, Midas found the courage to put his thoughts to words.

"Can I teach my words?" he asked, pointing to his throat. "Words of fire."

Elowen blinked, then smiled at him with softened eyes. "Yes, of course." Hope bloomed in Midas' chest, and he pondered for a moment of what he should teach her first.

Then, from his throat, came a sound not meant for human mouths. It was a rolling, guttural resonance that vibrated the very air between them. It echoed faintly against the stone walls. "Means heart."

"That's beautiful," she whispered. He kept his eyes on her, patiently waiting for her to try and mimic him. She opened her mouth, then paused, suddenly nervous. "Midas I don't think I can make those sounds."

He repeated it again, slower, then waited for her. "Try?" he asked softly.

Elowen swallowed, and then tried her best to mimic the shape of the word in her throat. She tried two, three times, but all that came out was a wheezing, hoarse cough. Her voice rasped and cracked over and over again, but eventually, they both realized that her tongue and throat simply weren't shaped to speak the language of the dragons.

Midas' expression was one of complete sorrow.

"Midas..." she said gently.

He lowered his head and closed his eyes. He was not angry, never angry at her, but it was a painful realization. He had so few things left from the age of the dragons, and this was just one more thing he could not share with another soul. It gutted him.

"I'm sorry," Elowen said, closing the distance between them and holding their hands together. "I wish I could speak your words, I truly do, but you don't need to teach me your words to share them with me. I understand you in different ways. Every time you look at me, or nuzzle me, or bring me food and trinkets, you speak. It's like a language we have all to ourselves. Isn't that beautiful?"

He looked at her, uncertain at first, but then her words began settling in. He simply nodded.

"Yes. Beautiful."

TWENTY-FOUR

THE FIRE CRACKLED low in the cave as twilight settled beyond the mouth of stone. Elowen sat with her knees tucked to her chest, watching Midas move around the hoard searching for comfort among the piles of things. He was in his dragon form tonight, curled protectively near the fire with his wings folded neatly against his sides, tail resting across the floor, the very tip rising and falling with his steady breaths.

She smiled softly as he reached for a length of velvet she had tucked over a rough pile of coins to make herself a proper seat. He adjusted it without being asked, smoothing it beneath her, then gave a low, pleased huff through his nose.

She had come to know these sounds. He didn't need words to tell her when he was content. It was in the way he pressed his snout against her side or curled his tail gently around her waist while she read aloud from the old books he'd rescued from ruined chapels.

Lately, he touched her more often. He used the very tip of his tail to stroke her cheek or her back. He nuzzled her with a kind of softness she had never known, not even in childhood. She'd learned that affection, for Midas, was through quiet, instinctive gestures.

She had been thinking lately about the way he showed affection to her, and how she could show it back. Rubbing the scales near his snout and snuggling into his tail at night simply didn't feel like enough compared to all he had done for her.

Something in her ached to show more human affection, but she was worried he would not understand. Midas kept one golden eye locked on her, sensing her desire to say something but not yet finding the words. She was nervous, he could tell, but whatever it was, he would understand.

"Midas? Can...can you shift for me?" she asked, already feeling guilty for it, knowing it caused him pain and left him exhausted.

But Midas did not hesitate. He moved to a safe distance away from her, and she waited patiently while he took his smaller human form. He came back to rejoin her side and tilted his head. Curious. Waiting.

His skin was streaked in faint scaled patterns, and she traced them along his collarbone. His hair fell in his face, but his golden reptilian eyes remained. They were still molten and watched her carefully.

"You don't have to stay like this long," she assured. "I just...wanted to try something." He said nothing. "You show me so much affection in your own way. I wanted to try something more...human. But I'm worried you might not like it."

He furrowed his brow, not quite understanding her. It sounded like nonsense to him. "I like it because it is from you."

He could hear her heart fluttering in her chest, confused why she had suddenly become so nervous. She had spoken of *affection*...but her behavior did not match. *Had he misunderstood? Had he displeased her in some way?*

Elowen reached out and brushed her fingertips along his jaw, and his breath hitched in the same way it always did when she touched him tenderly with her gentle hands. He blinked at her and gave her a small, encouraging nod. He trusted her, even if he didn't quite understand all of her words.

Elowen leaned in closer to him. It was slow enough that he could stop her or push her away, but he didn't. Her eyes closed just before he could feel her breath across his face, and then her lips touched his. It was...soft.

It was over in an instant. If he hadn't been so incessantly watching her, he might have even missed it, her mouth so featherlight on his.

He blinked at her when she pulled away, slightly started, slightly confused.

"That was a kiss," she said, her voice small and embarrassed. "Sometimes...humans do that when they want to thank someone they care for."

"Kiss." He looked at her lips, then at her eyes. "Strange," he murmured.

Instantly, her face fell. "I'm sorry, I shouldn't have—"

She began to pull away, and he reached out to keep her close. "No," he said, worrying he had displeased her. "Not bad, just not...dragon." He tilted his head to the side again, and used a finger to tilt her chin to meet his eyes. "It means thank you?"

She nodded. "Yes. But it can mean lots of things: affection, happiness, relief, love."

Love.

Midas' heart stuttered at that word. He stared at her for a long time, memorizing her lips that had so tenderly touched his.

He leaned forward slightly and cupped her cheek in his hand, mindful of his claws. His hand was far too large for her face, and it trembled as it tried to touch her with the same gentleness that came so easily when she touched him. Then, slowly, awkwardly, he leaned forward and pressed his lips to hers once more. It was clumsy. It was firmer than before, and their teeth scraped together at the action.

When he pulled away, he looked up at her with something shining in his eyes that Elowen had never seen, and within him, a feeling in his chest he had never felt.

Her cheeks turned pink, and Midas thought he had made a mess of the action. He stayed in his human form though, quietly hoping she would '*kiss*' him again.

Later, the scent of smoke and boiling meat filled the cave as she cooked herself supper. She had been feeding him small spoonfuls of the broth as she let it simmer in the pot over the fire. She had been trying to teach him the difference between flavors, to show him there was more to taste than raw meat. A pinch of salt here, a sprinkling of a peppery root there.

Midas insisted they were all the same.

Elowen simply laughed quietly, tasting the broth for herself once more and offering it to him again. He made a face at the small cube of meat that made its way onto the spoon, but dutifully took the bite.

His tongue pressed against the roof of his mouth, sucking the broth from the meat before chewing and swallowing. He narrowed his eyes on her.

"Sufficient," he murmured, simply to please her so that she would *stop* feeding it to him.

Elowen beamed at his simple word, radiant and full of life. The warmth in Midas' chest was greater than any fire he'd ever breathed.

Without thinking, without hesitating, he leaned forward and kissed her.

It was clumsy again. Their teeth bumped together, but it was filled with such an eager affection that Elowen let out a sound of surprise against his lips before melting into it.

He pulled back, his eyes wide and full of hope.

"Happy kiss," he said. "It was right?"

Elowen blinked once, a bit dazed and confused by his question. Then, suddenly, she was laughing. Midas stared, fascinated by the sound and how her hand covered her flushed face and her warm smile.

"Yes, yes Midas, that was perfect."

He eased back. His shoulders loosened. A smile tugged at the corner of his mouth. Her palm slid across his jaw and then she leaned in to kiss him again, softly this time. "It was perfect," she repeated.

He did not understand if he should do it again, or if he should save these kisses so as to not dilute their meaning, but he did know that smile on her face, and he craved it more than anything now, to keep her smiling like that because of something he did.

He leaned in again, slowly and deliberately this time. When their lips touched, her hands circled around his neck and his palms found her waist. He held her gently, so painfully aware of how fragile her marrow bones were, how soft her skin was.

But Elowen didn't seem afraid of the differences in them —not when she shifted and lifted her legs over his lap until she was seated against him. Her hands cupped his face and her thumbs swept across the remaining scales on his cheek.

She pulled away from his lips for a moment. "Do you trust me?" she whispered.

"Yes," he said. "*Yes*."

Carefully, so not to startle him, her fingers ran down his arms where rough patches of scales broke up his mostly human form. She traced the lines of his back where wing met muscle. Touched the very tips of the horns protruding from his skull. Kissed the tip of his nose.

All this time, Midas' hands never left her waist, but Elowen felt his hands pressing harder as she explored the upper planes of his chest.

She smiled softly. "You are so careful with me."

"I must be," he said immediately. "You are too breakable."

"Are you afraid of hurting me?"

"Yes."

Her thumb met his bottom lip, and she watched as she traced it before meeting his eyes again. "I'm not."

"Not breakable?" he asked.

"Not *afraid*."

Midas did not know what to do with that, and so a silence bloomed between them, but it was warm.

Elowen leaned forward again, but this time, she didn't kiss him. Instead, she buried her face in his neck and held him. He wrapped his arms around her with uncharacteristic gentleness, his hands sliding up and down her spine in steady lines.

He could feel the raised skin beneath her dress, of the marks the humans put on her. Anger flared in his chest, but he held her tighter and nuzzled into her hair with his human nose.

They stayed there like that, pressed heart-to-heart, while fire danced across the walls.

TWENTY-FIVE

MIDAS HAD KNOWN fire in every form. It was in his veins, in his throat, in his heart. He had felt it in his belly before a hunt, in his chest before battle, in his wings as he soared above cruel human villages.

But nothing in the world had prepared him for the fire that curled low in his spine as Elowen's fingers moved over his skin. She traced his back, pausing where each scale up his spine met his flesh. She studied it with her fingers, memorizing every groove and ridge.

She touched him as if he were sacred. Her hands were so small and delicate compared to him, and Midas often felt himself quietly drifting to sleep under her tender touches.

What cruelty it was, to put him under such a spell with nothing but a touch. It was unnatural for him to be so...soft; and yet he was for her.

Elowen heard the heavy rain from where they were lounging. It pounded against the cave mouth, and the wind howled as it snaked through the tunnels. A heavy gust reached them, but she simply hummed, content with the way none of it chilled her.

"You're so warm," she whispered against the top of Midas' head. He was resting with it against her chest, his hands splayed against her back, and their legs tangled together. His tail flicked at her voice.

He grumbled back to her, pleased, and whispered against her sternum. "I will always keep you warm."

She watched his tail move in a circular motion. She had learned that it was not just a part of his body, but it was a form of expression, too. It twitched when he was irritated, it swayed when he was relaxed, and it curled protectively around her like another arm whenever it could, like instinct more than conscious thought.

He sighed into her chest once more, then lifted his head to look at her. Something inside of him compelled him to kiss her, and so he pressed his lips to the underside of her chin. He wasn't sure what he was feeling. He didn't have the human words for it, but he knew that *she* made him feel it. His fingers left the underside of her and flipped them so he was the one now on his back.

She made a soft sound of surprise at the movement, but settled quickly on top of him, looking at him as if he had hung the stars in the sky for her. He caressed her cheek with the backside of his hand. Her lips found his palm.

What they were sharing was not passion the way the humans defined it. It was everything he didn't know he was craving after all those years of loneliness.

But Elowen had given it to him. She had always given him nothing but the best, most beautiful parts of her.

Her lips found the line of his jaw, the corner of his

mouth, and then settled over his. Midas kissed her with open eyes. He watched the way hers fluttered shut. He watched the flush rise to her cheeks. He felt her relax, bit by bit, as if laying down burdens he never knew she carried, trusting him to carry them for her.

When she pulled back, breathless and blinking, her smile was so gentle he thought he might die from it.

"You are beauty," he said to her.

"Beautiful?" she asked, correcting his usage of the word.

"No. You are *beauty*. You are all of beauty in this wretched world. My most precious treasure. My Elowen."

His hands moved, tentative against the curve of her hip, then the dip of her waist, then where her dress pulled taught against her chest. She sighed and moved slightly. Midas froze, worried he had hurt her.

"No," she murmured quickly. "It's okay. You can keep going."

He did.

His hands moved upward, exploring the shape of her back, her shoulders, her neck. He memorized every sound she made. The way she gasped when his fingers ran along the base of her skull and the way she melted when his thumbs passed the small of her back.

He committed it all to memory until it was etched into his mind as permanently as the mountain itself.

He reached for her hand and brought it to his mouth where he kissed each of her fingers and licked her palm. His fangs, the sharpness of his teeth leftover from his shift, scraped lightly against her skin, but she did not flinch.

His other hand traced back down her spine, one nail carefully drawing circles on her thigh just below her bum.

She squirmed against him, and it stirred something deep in him—something he had never felt before. He felt parts of his body stiffen that had never done so, and he suddenly moved her body off of his, ashamed and embarrassed at his reaction.

Elowen didn't understand at first, his sudden change in mood; not until she sat up and saw the heaviness between his human legs from a slit in his pelvis she hadn't noticed before.

"Oh," she said quietly, looking away to hide the pinkness in her cheeks.

"I am sorry," Midas told her, pulling a quilt over him to hide his shame. "I did not mean...I did not know."

"It's alright," Elowen said, finally meeting his eyes again. She rested her hand over his to assure him she was not mad.

"I did not mean to dishonor you," Midas said. "It is shameful for dragons to..." he could not find the words, for he was too embarrassed. "Such things are reserved for our mates. There is a ritual and it is sacred."

"I understand," she replied, nodding. "Maybe we should...sleep now."

"Yes, sleep," Midas agreed, though he had no intention of doing so in this smaller, human form. He moved away from her and shifted into his true dragon form where he was able to control his body easier. Elowen settled on the furs and blankets he had gathered for her, and Midas wrapped himself around her like he always did.

He did not sleep much that night, afraid his body had ruined what his heart treasured so deeply.

TWENTY-SIX

There had never been a need for sentiment in Midas' hoard. Not truly. He had amassed riches for decades—gilded chalices, painted ivory chess pieces, mirrors and hair pins. His talons had dug through riverbeds and ruined cities alike, hoarding the memories of the past.

But never had he had the desire to shape anything with his own claws.

Elowen had begun sleeping deeper in her nest, nestled into the curve of his tail, her breath warming the underside of his wing. She decorated their cave with stray flowers and old ribbons, wove bits of his hoard into little nooks and crannies that made the space feel less like a tomb and more like a home.

He didn't know what to give her in return. All earthly possessions seemed meaningless compared to what she had given him: purpose beyond fire, life beyond survival.

And then, one night, while patrolling a valley far beyond where he normally hunted, he saw a shimmer tucked into the roots of a half-dead tree. He landed and used his talons to drag it into the moonlight.

It was a stone, larger than the one he had given her before. It was a muted gray and veined with red and orange shimmer, like it had been kissed by his fire. It was a rough and imperfect stone, but it was perfect in the sense that it could be polished and carved just for Elowen.

Midas carried the stone back with his talons, careful not to crush or crack it. When he returned to the cave, Elowen was dreaming, and while she slept, he retreated deeper into the cave to quietly polish and carve the stone for her.

He tried with the tip of his talons first, but he found quickly that they were too large. Midas took a scale from his own body and shifted into his smaller human form. He sharpened the scale against the cavern walls, grinding it down until it was the perfect tool to etch patterns into the stone.

It took days, which turned into weeks, until he eventually stopped counting the time. He worked slowly and carefully, smoothing every jagged edge and polishing the stone to the perfect shine.

In the stone, he mimicked Elowen's frame the best he could. Next to her, he carved a more draconic one. Their heads were bowed close, unified as one.

Midas finally approved of what he had carved, and ran his claws over the final piece. He held it gently in his human palms, and wondered if Elowen would see everything he had carved that he didn't have the words for.

He approached Elowen's sleeping form and tucked the stone under a pile of coins, where he would keep it until the right moment to present it to her.

He didn't have to wait long.

He sat awake deep in the night a few days later, polishing the stone again in the firelight. It wasn't because of anything she did, but Midas looked down at the stone and was suddenly overwhelmed by something unfamiliar. It was a tightness in his chest, a trembling down his spine, and a craving for attention that could only be sated by Elowen.

And he had carved this stone for her to tell her those things, but more than that, he knew the human word now, and that was what he wanted to tell her most of all: that he loved her.

The realization struck him like lightning. He needed her —and it was more than protection or instinct. It was like survival, like he needed her voice, her smell, her soul intertwined with his.

Midas had lived in solitude for so long, and had thought he would continue living that way. But now he knew that he could live on only with her at his side.

As if sensing his nerves, Elowen began to stir in her sleep. Midas leaned over her, nuzzling his nose into her hair and stroking her cheek to settle her once more. She sighed softly and went still once more. He tightened his tail around her and simply watched her sleep.

A human girl, surrounded by his hoard and the warmth of his undeniable love for her. She was his entire world.

Tomorrow, he would give her the stone and ask her to be his in the way that the ancient dragons proposed a union. Not his as a possession nor a prize, but a mate—a partner. His heart.

By morning, the fire had dwindled to soft coals. Midas

did not have the strength to leave Elowen's embrace to strengthen the fire with his breath. He sat quietly until she woke naturally, and stayed quiet as she prepared breakfast for herself and bathed.

Elowen didn't mind the silence. Their companionship had long since grown past the need for constant talk. His words were in the way he curled around her, the way he shared his warmth and cared for her. Somehow, she knew that his actions could express his feelings better than any words in her tongue or his own.

After her bath, as she brushed her long hair with an ivory comb sitting atop a thick velvet cloth, Midas watched in his larger dragon form and fidgeted nervously. She noticed, but did not push him to say something he wasn't ready for. She filled the silence by humming a tune, knowing he enjoyed it.

The golden shimmer of his scales caught the firelight, and his powerful muscles rippled with each tense movement. He slowly began to approach her, his head lowered just above the floor. He stayed like that, motionless before her.

Elowen blinked. "Midas?"

He crooned softly in acknowledgement, and then uncurled the talons to present her with the stone.

She observed it for a moment. It was not like the other stones he had gathered for her. This one was dark and streaked with fiery colors. It had been carefully polished into a perfect oval, and along its surface was carved deep scratches that created the shape of a girl and a dragon.

He set it gently on the stone ground of the cave and moved back slightly, giving her space to observe it. She stared at it, brushing her fingers over the carvings before her breath caught in her throat.

"What is this?" she asked, voice trembling. "You made this?"

He pressed his snout to her chest and then bowed his head as close to the ground as he could manage. It was a gesture as old as time itself, and given only once.

To a mate.

Elowen didn't understand that significance. How could she? But Midas also knew that if he were to ask her to stay with him, to be his mate, that he had to do it properly as the old ways would require.

The proposal is meant to be as meaningful as the life they are to share together; it could not be rushed, nor could it be completed properly in the human tongue.

Midas lifted his head slowly, trembling with vulnerability that Elowen could see but that he scarcely understood himself.

You are my treasure, Elowen. My fire. My life. My home, Midas said in his mother tongue. *I do not know your words well enough to understand how humans do this, but I know what dragons do. You are not dragon, but I am yours, and so I offer you this unity stone, for I cannot give you my beating heart.*

Elowen, always paying attention, knew he was offering something significant. This was not just a gift as the others were. Then, her mind wandered momentarily to a few nights prior, to when he spoke of rituals and mates and how sacred such things were to the dragons.

Her mouth fell open. Tears gathered in her eyes so fast she did not have time to blink them away. Elowen's hand flew to her mouth and a sob broke from her chest, overwhelmed by the emotions she was feeling.

Midas mistook her crying for pain or discomfort, and tried to gently pry the stone from her hands with his talons as carefully as possible. She snatched it away. "No!" she yelped. "Don't take it, please. It's the most beautiful thing I've ever seen."

Midas' head tilted from side to side, almost childlike in his confusion.

She reached up, hands trembling, and pressed her palm to his snout while holding the stone to her chest. "You carved *us*."

He inhaled sharply as he watched her tears fall freely down her cheeks, dripping onto the stone and his scales. He leaned in slowly, afraid to frighten her, and pressed his enormous forehead to hers. She pulled him closer and closer until she was practically laying on his snout, bent at the waist with her small arms embracing his face.

His breath hitched. His wings trembled. Her tears gathered on his scales into one large drop before gravity pulled it down his face. He caught it with his talon before it hit the ground and swiped it away with his tongue. He could taste the raw emotion in her tears; the love, the trust, the longing.

When she finally pulled away, Midas slowly shifted to his human form. He knelt beside her, but didn't immediately speak. He just took her hand and maneuvered their fingers so that they traced the stone together.

"This is my vow," he finally said, voice hoarse from the shift. "It is...the words I do not yet know how to say. The hope in my heart that you will stay with me. To be mate. It means more than hatchlings. To dragons, mate means eternity. Always. Forever."

Midas knelt, staring at her searching for some reaction that would tell him if he was doing this right. He had no cultural understanding of how humans asked these things, nor did he know the ceremony or language for it—but he understood Elowen in ways the humans never had, and so he hoped that she would accept it—accept *him*.

Elowen gently set the stone down in her nest, then knelt with him. She took his clawed hands in both of hers.

She gazed deep into his molten eyes, and whispered: "I shall love you until long after all the stars in the skies burn out."

A sound escaped him—relief and astonishment. "Do you mean it, Elowen?" he asked, reaching for her cheek.

"More than I've ever meant anything in my life."

He pressed their foreheads together again, unable to look at her, for his gratitude was too great. Then, he kissed her.

And he finally understood why she had told him that humans kiss to show love. For what other action could feel so natural to give in a moment of happiness?

"I love you, Elowen."

Elowen's voice broke when she answered. "Say it again."

He did. Then again. Until it was no longer a word, but a promise.

They stayed like that until the fire faded and the night deepened. And when she laid her head against his chest and whispered that she would stay with him for all her days, Midas held her like the only treasure in the world he could never bear to lose.

TWENTY-SEVEN

IT WAS the middle of the rainy season, and the downpour had left the mouth of the cave damp and cold. Elowen stood just out of reach of the water, barefoot, letting the soothing smell of rain cling to her.

Behind her, Midas stood in the shape of a man, his hair long down his back. His feet were heavy against the stone as he approached. Elowen didn't turn, not right away at least. She simply stayed in place, watching the rain, and felt Midas' heat at her back.

His hand rose to brush her loose hair away from her neck, and tenderly kissed the curve where it met her shoulder. She turned to face him.

His eyes, golden as the dawn, met hers like they always did—like he could never quite believe that she was real. Even now. Even after he had asked her to be his and all the weeks since.

Midas saw something new in her eyes, but he wasn't sure what it was.

They had never been good at hiding things from each other. Not worry, nor care, nor the way their bodies had been...*passionate* for each other as of late.

But they had never been ready. Not until now, like the softness of the rain whispered to them that it was finally the right moment.

Elowen took his hand and led him into the cave wordlessly, past the hearth where she cooked meals and into the alcove where their nest was.

They spoke no words, for there were none needed. Elowen let her hands trace the lines of him—the curve of his shoulders, the scales down his spine, across his abdomen.

And when he touched her, it was with the same tenderness.

Midas had told Elowen before that this sort of intimacy was reserved for the sacred bond of mates. He had been careful to respect Elowen and her body, never touching her until he received her invitation.

He explored every curve of her body like a map he was committing to memory. Like a riddle he was waiting to find the answer to. He did not rush, he savored.

Her sighs were every answer he had ever wanted to hear.

They quickly knew what brought the other pleasure, and moved like the tides are drawn to the moon. Elowen's fingers tangled in his dark hair and Midas' lips found every bare piece of her, mixing their scents until they were indistinguishable from one another.

Afterward, they lay together on the furs and quilts of

their nest, bare in every way. Not dragon and human, but lovers and loved.

Midas kissed her again, and she opened for him once more. As his body moved against hers in a beautiful, steady rhythm, Elowen wrapped her arms around him and whispered his name.

His entire body shuddered.

Outside, the rain continued to fall, but inside, the cave burned with firelight and passion—two hearts joining for the first time in sacred intimacy they had unknowingly saved for each other.

MORNING CAME SLOW, like honey from a jar. The cave was still and humidity clung to the stones.

Elowen stirred first, but Midas tightened his tail, still curled around her legs from the night before. He did not want her to retreat from the lingering beauty and fragile spell of the night they shared together. Her bare skin was warm against his, some of his scales leaving patterns into her flesh from holding her so close to him all night.

Her body still hummed from soreness and memory of Midas' body sharing hers. The memory of the way he had looked at her like she was something worth worshiping.

His eyes were still closed, but Elowen turned her head slightly to face him. She pressed a kiss to the underside of his jaw, and only then did he open his golden eyes.

He blinked slowly, as if contemplating if it had all been

a dream. His eyes traced down the nakedness of them both, and Elowen felt her cheeks flush.

"Good morning," she whispered.

Midas tilted his head towards her and nuzzled her. That was his primary way of communicating with her. Not with words, but with touch, with tenderness.

He paused and then sat up slightly, reaching a hand toward her as if he were uncertain if he was still allowed to touch her. His fingers brushed her hair away from her shoulder and then trailed down the length of her arm. When she didn't flinch away or tell him to stop, he continued to trace her body as gently as he could manage.

When he got to the underside of the curve of her breast, Midas made a soft sound in his throat, like a purr. "Elowen..." he trailed off, voice unsure. "Did I hurt you?"

She sighed, her heart aching with the knowledge that he was always concerned for her above all else. "No, Midas. It was perfect."

That seemed to ease something in him, and he smiled awkwardly in return.

"What?" Elowen asked.

"Again?" he asked eagerly. She had to stifle a laugh as she turned beet red. She knew it was probably just instinct for him, but he was after all, an animal. She didn't mean it in a bad way, just that his body worked in different ways than hers, and she wasn't sure she could handle another day of...*that* just yet.

Instead of trying to explain, she nodded, just once, and reached for his hand. "Soon," she promised.

He made that low sound again—satisfied and affectionate. He nuzzled her once more before they untangled their limbs.

Elowen retreated to a chamber further back in the cave where a large copper basin of water waited for her. It functioned as her bath, and she stepped into the water, cleaning away the blood and Midas' passion from her thighs.

When she finished her bath, Midas helped her dress, though he grew frustrated with the ties at the back and let her do it herself. He had prepared a simple breakfast for her of berries, flatbread, and dried meat. Soon after she finished, the exhaustion of his human form caught up to him, and Midas involuntarily returned to his natural dragon shape, quickly falling into a deep slumber near her nest.

The rest of the day was spent tidying the cave. Midas had a tendency to trek dirt and mud, and so Elowen brushed away what she could with a broom she fashioned out of a large stick and a bundle of dried grass. Then she dragged a bucket of dirty water to the cave mouth for Midas to replace the next time he went to the lake.

Elowen never asked to go back, not because she didn't want to, but because she was afraid. It was too close to her old village, and the scars on her back, though healed, were still new. She did miss the fresh air and foraging, but she simply wasn't ready for what might be waiting for them there.

After her chores, Elowen relaxed near the cooking fire, preparing a broth for her supper. Elowen didn't have much opportunity in the village to cook. Most of their meals were rations of thin, mushy gruel. But here with Midas, he brought her so much food that she had noticeably gained weight, and her stomach no longer ached with hunger as it used to. She had a collection of herbs and spices and aromatics she could experiment with. It was simple, but it breathed life into her that she didn't realize she was missing in her old life.

She didn't realize how many mundane things, like cooking, had been taken from her in exchange for peace and order.

It was after her supper when Midas finally woke with a grumble that gently shook the cave. His eyes found her instantly, and he dipped his head in acknowledgement as he stretched his wings from wall to wall.

Elowen asked him to join her at the mouth of the cave. The clouds had momentarily broken, and though the rain left the stones wet, she sat with Midas curled around her. She pointed at the sky and told him of the constellations that painted the heavens.

Midas thought they were dull in comparison to his Elowen's eyes, but he listened anyway. He loved learning of these silly human things like stories in the stars from her. He loved knowing that, through all the cruelty she had witnessed with the humans, she still found beauty in the world.

Midas hummed, nuzzling her with the side of his snout and dragging the very tip of his forked tongue against her cheek.

I shall take you to the stars, my Elowen.

She didn't ask him what he said, and he didn't need to tell her. He would show her, one day.

She fell asleep there, curled into his chest, and Midas smiled into the dark.

TWENTY-EIGHT

A MONTH PASSED, and for a fortnight, Midas had been having strange dreams. They were brief and meaningless, but always woke him with unease that vanished the moment his lids lifted.

He had believed he felt the air shifting, but he could not explain it. Something was wrong, but it also wasn't. He could smell it.

It wasn't wrong in a dangerous way. It wasn't like the stink of a human or steel. What he sensed was older. Primal.

It bothered Midas so much that night that he stirred from the nest. He rose with a low rumble and lowered his head, sniffing the ground. No vermin. No spoiled meat.

Still, the scent gnawed at him, at his instincts. He was restless as he searched for the source, careful to stay quiet and mind Elowen's slumber. She needn't worry about such things, he would find the source and see it gone before she woke.

Midas blinked slowly, adjusting his eyes to the dim light of the cave, looking for movement. The cave smelled as it always did—woodsmoke and Elowen clung to the walls—but something beneath all of it was different. He lowered his head again to the ground and inhaled.

He closed his eyes and trusted his nose to carry him forward. He paused only when the tip of his snout bumped the fur-lined nest Elowen slept in.

He tilted his head in confusion, and breathed in her scent. He could detect no sickness under her skin, nor did she smell of filth. She simply smelled…different.

She lay curled into herself, tucked under a quilt she had stitched herself with old clothing she had found amongst his treasures. She breathed steadily and he could see no distress on her face. Nothing about her seemed different.

Then he noticed her heartbeat was faster than usual. Her sleep was deeper. She radiated more warmth than before.

He lowered his snout and took in her scent once again, just to be certain it was her. Indeed, the scent lived there. Not just in her hair or on her skin nor her clothes. It was delicate and distinct, but it seemed to emanate from inside her.

He sniffed again, and his eyes shot open instantly. He cowered away from her, bumping against the cave wall in his panic. He recognized the scent from deep within his memories, from a time when his own mother was heavy with the eggs of his brothers and sisters.

Life. Not hers, but another life that fluttered beneath her skin. His body grew tense. It was life that they had created together. He knew it with the same certainty as he knew he loved her.

Elowen carried his child.

Days passed. Midas said nothing. Elowen continued her routines as normal, but Midas watched her with a new caution—followed her like he was on a lead attached to her belly.

He watched as she slept longer. He watched as her appetite changed. Some mornings she barely ate. Others, she would ask for things she had never craved before. He watched as her skin flushed with heat so intense she had to put a wet rag to her forehead for relief. All of these things, she didn't notice herself, or perhaps she thought it was just a mild sickness.

She never complained. And she didn't know what Midas knew, but he had already become overwhelmed with what needed to be done. Every part of him bristled with the ancient drive to protect, to prepare, to comfort.

Elowen was carrying their future, and no one would touch her. Not the humans, not fate, not even time. He would bring her more food, more furs, more water, more clothes. He would make sure she understood how significant this was.

As she hummed to herself and stirred broth in a pot, he lowered himself beside her, one heavy wing at her back, and his massive golden eye watching her every move.

And Midas, the ancient and fearsome and terrifying creature that he was, listened to her and the tiny heartbeat in her belly that accompanied her song like a drum.

MIDAS HAD ALWAYS BEEN PROTECTIVE. Elowen had long grown used to his silent shadow behind her. A hidden presence to all except her. She'd even grown accustomed to waking with his wings half-curled around her, his warmth a shield against their mountain's chill.

But now...

Now he didn't just follow. He...hovered. Watched her every step as if the ground might crack beneath her. Every time she moved too quickly, he rumbled low in his throat. His eyes stayed trained on her hands, her posture, her breath.

It was beginning to worry her. He was watching her like she was destined for the grave—like he was waiting for her to collapse.

He wouldn't let her lift the water skin. Wouldn't let her carry her satchel. Wouldn't even let her bathe alone. And when she tried to ask him why, he only blinked and turned away, as if ashamed to answer.

Elowen sat at the mouth of the cave one morning, absently toying with the ends of her hair that had grown soft and shiny with regular washes.

She had been tired lately. Her chest ached for no reason. Her dreams were full of strange colors. Her body felt swollen. As time went on, she had begun to think that Midas really did have reason to be concerned for her.

She heard the scrape of his claws behind her, and

turned to watch as he approached slowly with his head dipped low. His wings were tucked tight to his back as if trying to make himself smaller. He came right to her, eyes glowing faintly, and nudged her cheek with the end of his snout.

"Something is wrong," she whispered. Midas tensed, and tilted his head—a sign that he was listening. "Not with *me*. With you. You've been acting like the wind will shatter me."

He stepped forward another half-pace and wrapped his tail all the way around her. She sat on the thick muscle, awaiting some sort of explanation. When he did not indicate he would change into his human form to speak, Elowen's heart ached. He looked at her as if he were memorizing every line of her face.

Then, slowly, deliberately, Midas lowered his great snout to her stomach. His breath paused for a moment before he gave a single exhale and gently nudged her belly with the tip of his nose.

Elowen froze. "What?"

His golden eyes lifted to hers, and he blinked, waiting for her to put the pieces together herself. A hand flew to her stomach. She blinked at him, her breath trembling and heart pounding.

"That's not possible," she whispered, trying to deny what he and her body were quietly telling her. "I...I don't understand."

Midas nuzzled against her once more, a sign of great affection, and let her process what was happening in silence. Neither of them had ever heard of such a thing—a human and a dragon conceiving a child. But Elowen knew that Midas' senses would not deceive him, and that from his behavior, he had likely known for weeks.

Elowen laughed out a broken, stunned sound that turned into a soft sob, accompanied by a smile that went up to her eyes. Midas made a low, apologetic noise. He never liked to see her cry, even if it was from happiness.

She leaned forward and pressed her forehead to his, hand still over her belly. "You knew," she whispered. "You've been taking care of me. *Us.*"

His eyes fluttered closed. For a long moment, they simply stayed like that: woman, dragon, and the tender life in her belly.

TWENTY-NINE

Elowen didn't expect things to happen so quickly after she found out she was carrying Midas' child.

One day, she could still curl beside him at night, her knees tucked comfortably beneath her chin. The next, her dress clung tight across her hips and strained at the seams. Midas had always fed her well, and her body that was once worn thin by starvation already grew the curves of abundance—but now her body grew round and full with a swiftness that startled them both.

It had scarcely been two months and Elowen looked halfway to bursting.

It was not human, this pregnancy. That should have been obvious, given the circumstances, but it was a marvel and a curse at the way her body changed so quickly. Her ankles and joints complained at every movement. Her skin was too often flushed. Her stomach was always unsettled and emptied itself before every meal. Her muscles felt weak and useless. She moved slower and needed more rest.

Midas had become anew—a creature of vigilance and tenderness. No longer did he bring her shiny baubles from his outings. Now he brought softer bedding, finer clothes, and an abundance of offerings for the child. Wood-carved bassinets, toys, blankets, clothes.

He didn't sleep much anymore. Always too worried, always watching, always needing to provide and support.

When Elowen vomited, he cleaned her face. When the aches in her joints brought her to tears, he cradled her with his tail. He only gave her the freshest, cleanest water he had melted from the tip of the mountain, and everything she ate went through a thorough inspection under his nose to ensure it was safe and fresh.

He cared for her like he always had: as something precious, but with a new ferocity built on instinct.

Whenever Elowen tried to do anything for herself, even as simple as stirring soup, Midas would block her path with a frown, rumbling from his chest until she sat back down. Guilt shown in his eyes from confining her to the nest, but he would not risk anything happening to her or the child.

When sleep found her, Midas stayed awake. He watched her, but he also made it a habit to croon against her belly, where their child grew with a strange, relentless speed.

Midas had great worry that this child might see him as a monster, and his hope is that they would recognize the sound when they were born, and understand that there was no creature alive that would keep them safer.

Elowen awoke one night to his crooning, his golden eyes meeting hers and softening. She glanced down at her swollen belly and back up. "They are growing so fast. Too fast, maybe. I'm not sure my body will hold them for much longer. I might give birth before the next full moon."

He had made the same assumption weeks ago, but did not answer her.

And he certainly did not tell her how much it worried him.

WHEN MORNING CAME, Midas had gone to fetch more food. If Elowen began her labor soon, he was unsure of how long it would be before he was able to hunt again. She had taught him how to salt and preserve meat, how to seal clay pots to keep fruit fresh, and how to purify water with fire if needed. All of these things he could now do with practiced ease in his human form, though the stress from Elowen's discomfort made it hard for him to shift.

He returned to the mouth of the cave quietly. The mountain had grown warm with the rising sun, and Elowen was already awake, peeling an orange in the nest.

He had not meant to hide, but found himself listening to her soft voice echoing faintly against the stone, lilting like birdsong. He paused just beyond a bend in the passage.

Fire lit her face, and her hair was unbound over her shoulder. Her voice was low—a hush meant for no one but the child nestled safely in her womb.

Or so she thought—for Midas crouched in the shadows and listened.

"You know," she murmured, running her fingers in slow

circles over her stomach, "your father is the most remarkable thing I've ever known."

He stilled, breath caught tight in his throat.

"I don't know how he's real," she whispered. "Sometimes, I wonder if I dreamt him. That I fell asleep in the woods one day and imagined all of this. My people call him a monster. But he's no such thing. Not really. Not to me." She paused, her voice growing softer. "He loves fiercely. I don't know if he truly knows what love means in my tongue, but he still shows it. I see it in everything he does. Every time he feeds me. Every time he shields me from the world. Every time he curls around us like he's daring anything to try and take us from him."

Midas' chest ached. He hadn't realized how tightly he'd curled his claws into the stone until a tremble passed through them. Her words pressed into him like a new fire in his chest. She had never spoken these things to his face. Never told him he was kind. Or brave. Or precious. He didn't know how to hold those truths.

"I hope you have his eyes," Elowen said quietly, voice full of warmth. "They're gold like sunlight. Like he swallowed the dawn. I want you to look at the world with those eyes one day and know that you're loved. That even if the world doesn't understand you, he will. I will."

Midas moved without thinking. A quiet shuffle of his weight. Elowen turned toward the sound—and there he was, caught in the dim glow of firelight, golden eyes wide, his expression unreadable in the flicker of shadows.

Midas stepped forward, slow and careful. He didn't speak. The words would never be enough, even if he found them. Instead, he lowered his head beside her and pressed his snout ever so gently against her swollen belly, breathing in the scent of her skin and the new life beneath it. A promise passed between them in that breathless moment —silent, but steady.

He would protect them. He would never stop. Elowen touched his jaw, soft and reverent.

"You heard me?" she asked.

He nodded once, and though she did not know it, he had already committed every word to memory—another precious treasure carved into his heart.

THIRTY

Midas stirred before the dawn.

The cave was quiet. Eerily so. The usual rhythm of Elowen's breathing was there, but beneath it pulsed a shift in the air, something only he could sense. It prickled along his scales like static, ancient instincts stirring in the marrow of his bones.

He lifted his head slowly from where he had coiled himself around the edges of the nest, careful not to rouse her. Elowen slept fitfully now. The weight of their unborn child rested heavy in her belly, and her discomfort had worsened by the day. Midas had noticed the way she winced when she turned, the way her breath would catch mid-sentence, and how she barely touched her food except when he fussed and fed her himself.

Midas reached out with his nose, pressing it gently to her bare shoulder. Her skin was hot. Elowen's labor was close. Though she had only been growing the child for less than half of the time of a human pregnancy, her body was already preparing for birth.

He rose in silence, transforming quickly and with strain into his two-legged form—still scaled, still winged, still not quite human, but small enough to move through the narrow alcoves of the cavern without his tail knocking over the drying herbs and bones lining the walls. His body ached from the change, but he bore it. For her.

There was water to heat. The smoothest of the river stones he had gathered earlier were placed into the fire to warm the basin. Blankets were unfurled and spread around the nest, shaken and fluffed and scented with her flowers. A half-cooked stew was stirred back to life with a bit of dried meat and wild greens he had foraged, just in case she could stomach it after.

And still...it did not feel like he had done enough. Not when she carried something so precious in her womb, and when the unknown was quickly creeping up on them.

Thoughts of the labor worried him often—he worried if Elowen would even survive birthing a half-dragon child in whatever form they might take.

His taloned hands shook as he placed jars of salves within arm's reach of the bedding. He knew these herbs well now—Elowen had taught him. He knew what eased pain, what slowed bleeding, what cooled fever. He would give her everything she needed. He would *not* lose her.

Midas paused at the edge of the firelight, his golden eyes flicking to Elowen's sleeping form. His tail lashed slowly, restlessly behind him.

Then—her breath caught. A whimper broke from her throat, sharp and raw. Midas was at her side in an instant.

"Elowen," he whispered, his voice rough.

She gasped. The pain came like fire in her spine. Her hand flew to her belly, and her eyes shot open wide and wet.

"Midas," she choked, voice strangled. "Something is happening—"

A wave of pain hit her unlike anything she had ever felt before. Her body curled forward, wracked with the first full contraction. Midas caught her before she could fall forward, holding her gently in arms that felt suddenly too large, too clumsy, too unworthy.

"Elowen. Safe. Breathe," he repeated, again and again, low and soft into her hair. She clung to him, teeth gritted, tears falling fast down her cheeks.

"I'm scared," she whispered.

He kissed her brow. "No fear. I am here."

She nodded, her whole body trembling with emotion and pain and uncertainty.

And then the night swallowed them whole, labor beginning in earnest, pain cresting and falling like waves in a storm—and Midas, beast of fire and claw, became a cradle of gentleness. He knelt beside her through every cry, every breath, every trembling squeeze of her fingers around his.

The pain grew worse by the second, and Elowen began screaming. Not the delicate kind she'd heard in birth stories whispered by village midwives, but an *animal* scream, ripped from her chest as her body heaved and cracked and stretched in ways it was never meant to, to deliver something the world had never seen before.

Her knees slipped on the pelts soaked with sweat, her hands grasping for anything solid—only to find the ridged curve of Midas' human forearm. She dug her fingers in until his skin split and blood streaked his scales. He didn't flinch. He would let her rip his bones from his hide if she needed to.

He wiped her brow. He murmured nonsense words in the dragon tongue. He growled at the shadows as if they dared come closer.

But as her labor intensified, and her distress filled his chest, Midas found it nearly impossible to hold himself in his human form for her. He changed back to his natural shape almost against his will, barely managing to move to a safe distance away from her.

Useless, Midas scolded himself. *Worthless!*

His claws scored gouges deep into the floor where he gripped it to keep still so that she could grip and claw at him herself. Elowen screamed again, tearful words escaping her throat.

"I can't do this!" she shouted.

Midas let out a low, guttural sound. *Helplessness.* His tail coiled and uncoiled beside her, snapping like a struck whip. He wanted to shift, to hold her with the hands she trusted, but her agony burned through the bond between them like lightning. He couldn't steady himself long enough to change.

"I'm *dying*, Midas," she gasped, collapsing into herself once more. Her body shook uncontrollably. "I swear to the old gods, *I'm dying!*"

He flinched from the grief in her voice. Another contraction hit. Her whole body seized. She clawed at his scales again, her broken fingernails scraping until there were no scales left and she gripped at his sensitive hide.

If pain was all he could give her now—he would offer it. He bowed his head so close that her blood smeared along his snout, her screams echoing inside the cage of his skull.

"Why would you do this to me?" she wept, but the words trembled. "It hurts...I can't do it! I'm not strong enough."

Her voice cracked on the last word, swallowed by another surge of pressure deep inside her. She curled forward again, howling like a wounded creature, and Midas bellowed with her, unable to do *anything* except stay.

The labor went on. Time lost meaning.

He did not know how to help, but he understood she was in pain.

And he could do nothing but watch.

Blood slicked her thighs. Her hair clung to her face. Her lips were dry and cracked from panting. Every time she tried to rest, another wave of pain crashed through her, leaving her shivering and soaked in fear.

Midas didn't move an inch away from her.

"You're going to break me," she whispered once between contractions, voice hollow. "This child is going to split me in two. I won't survive, Midas."

Her courage was faltering, and he could feel it. When her body was ready to push, she braced before trying with everything she had.

The scream she let out tore something *inside* him.

Blood and heat and fluid spilled onto the stone. Her thighs shook violently, and Midas rose slightly, panic blazing through him.

But then—

A sound. A shrill, wet *wail* filled the cave.

Elowen slumped back, shaking, pale, barely conscious —but *alive*.

Beneath her, between her legs, lay a child. *Their* child.

Midas froze. The air around him stilled. Elowen's head lolled weakly, eyes fluttering open just enough to find the child. She sobbed and reached for her new son with hands that shook so badly she couldn't lift him.

Midas moved, finally.

He nosed the child forward gently with his snout, guiding him to Elowen's chest. She curled around the boy with the last strength she had left.

"I did it," she whispered, dazed.

And then, another wave of pain hit her so intensely that she nearly lost grip of her child. Midas was there, of course. He caught the wriggling, slimy newborn with his tail, holding him steady against her chest.

Midas leaned his head down to inspect Elowen's body, to see what was there that could be causing her more pain. She seized once more, and when she did, Midas saw it— another child crowning between her legs, forcing itself into the world.

Her body trembled with exhaustion, blood pooling beneath her. Midas made a low, desperate sound—his talons digging into the stone beneath them. He would have given her his fire, his heart, anything to take her pain as she brought another babe into the world.

The second child came with a sudden rush, limbs limp but breathing. Elowen collapsed, eyes fluttering closed for a terrifying moment before her chest rose again.

He helped lift the child into her arms as he did the first one, and only once Elowen's breathing steadied did he bend his head forward to examine the newborns. Both males. Both strong in their breath and warm with fire in their hearts—Midas could feel it as easily as he could feel his own.

He sniffed, then opened his mouth and drew his tongue across the firstborn's skin, clearing the afterbirth with precise, delicate strokes. It was instinct more than thought. The second child received the same. He licked them clean, pressed his muzzle to their damp heads, breathing in the scent of them like it might brand them to his soul.

They were tiny. Fragile. Yet unmistakably marked by him. Their eyes gleamed with that same molten gold that burned in his.

He made a low, thrumming sound in his chest. Something protective. Something proud. Elowen stirred weakly, eyes fluttering open. He turned to her.

She was pale, soaked in sweat, hair tangled against her cheeks, but she was alive. He curled beside her, careful not to disturb the blood-streaked blankets, and pressed his snout gently to her shoulder.

"I'm...I'm okay," she whispered, though her voice was barely above a whisper. Her fingers found the edge of his face, stroking the warm scales there.

The twins squirmed in the curve of her arm. She looked down at them—two tiny boys, their skin pink and flushed, each one bearing the mark of their father in his eyes.

Midas made a low sound and curled his wings protectively around all three of them. He lowered his head until it rested beside hers, his gold eyes soft and wide with awe.

Together, they breathed in the quiet. In that moment, there was no world beyond the cave. Only a woman, a dragon, and two newborn boys—held together with fire and love. Their cave, their home, once a tomb of silence and solitude, came alive with the sound and scent of family, legacy, and pride.

THE FIRE CRACKLED LOW, casting a soft glow over the curve of the cave's interior. Outside, a wet, cold storm whispered against the stone, but within, all was warm.

Midas lay coiled along the outer edge of their den, his massive form at rest, though his eyes were not closed.

They were on *them.*

Elowen sat on a pile of fur-lined blankets, back braced against a mound of softened pelts, her legs curled beneath her. One of the twins, the more impatient one, was nestled against her chest, his tiny fists balled tightly near his face, mouth latched to her breast.

Midas didn't move for long stretches, and his breath was slow and deep, as though afraid that even exhaling too loud might disrupt the moment.

Elowen murmured something low and sweet as she smoothed the baby's dark hair. Her clothing had been ripped and soiled during the birth, so she removed it entirely, but she seemed unbothered; natural, content, and utterly focused on her sons.

Midas had seen the rawness of childbirth, the fire of her pain. He had seen blood and trembling and strength that rivaled the mountains. But this quiet act of nourishment, of giving not just safety but sustenance, was something else entirely. It was beautiful.

He inched closer, just enough to see better, not daring to touch or interfere. His wing curled inward, a barrier between them and the rest of the world.

Elowen noticed him watching. "You can come closer," she said, patting the nest near her side.

Midas hesitated, then moved with slow grace, lowering his head beside her. He didn't speak, but rested his snout close enough to feel the warmth of her skin and the steady heartbeat of his son. When the first had finished feeding, she gently traded places with the second in her lap in order to feed him as well.

Elowen smoothed the baby's back, rocking gently. "I never thought I'd be doing this in a cave. With a dragon." He let out a soft sound, deep in his throat. Not offended. Thoughtful. "But you're not just a dragon, are you?" she added quickly, glancing at him. "You're...you're their father."

He blinked, slow and heavy. His eyes lowered to her chest again—her body so small, so human, and yet she did what no magic of his could ever do. She fed them. She grew them. She birthed them with an animalistic grace and beauty he felt unworthy to witness.

He watched her fingers move. The way she shifted the baby's weight. The way her thumb soothed a crease in his brow. He studied everything.

He'd never seen anything so fragile or so powerful.

When both boys had finished nursing, Elowen held them both to her shoulders, rocking them gently. The infants gave contented sighs in sync with each other, eyes drifting shut.

She looked at Midas with a kind of tired triumph.

Midas reached forward—slow, careful—and placed the tip of one claw lightly beside one of the newborn's feet, as if measuring the size of his own children.

They will be strong, he said softly in a language his mate could not understand, but Elowen smiled and nodded as if she had.

Though he could not nurse, or cradle, or hum lullabies the way she did, Midas vowed in that quiet moment to learn every other thing she needed.

Because she had given their children life, and he would give them everything else.

THIRTY-ONE

After the birth, the world was a haze of pain and soft breath. The bliss of fresh newborn children had worn off, and Elowen grew tired, weak, and irritated.

She drifted in and out of sleep, her body too battered to rest, too exhausted to wake. Every inch of her felt torn open. Her womb ached with an emptiness that had once been full of fire and life. Her thighs trembled uncontrollably. Her chest burned as two small mouths suckled, demanding strength she no longer had.

Still, she endured. The twins were bundled against her skin, warm and fragile. She held one against each breast, cradled them with arms that barely obeyed her.

Her lips were dry. Her eyes crusted. Blankets clung damp to her skin—still soaked with blood, sweat, and the strange fluid that had spilled from her during the long hours of labor. She whimpered softly as a cramp rolled through her lower belly, the aftermath of delivery still wracking her with aftershocks.

A claw, gentle as breath, nudged her shoulder. Midas had finally regained enough control of himself to shift back to his human form. He pressed a bowl of cool water to her lips and supported her neck with his tail as she drank, his touch careful. She could barely swallow, her throat raw, but she tried. He coaxed her with soft sounds, brushing strands of hair back from her temple, wiping sweat from her brow with the corner of a cloth she recognized from his hoard.

When she coughed, he stilled. Waited. Breathed with her, then brought another bowl to her mouth.

"Eat," he whispered, voice cracked and guttural from disuse. "Please."

Broth touched her lips over the rim of the bowl. Salty, rich, and warm against her tongue. Though every swallow felt like a mountain, she knew in order to nourish her sons, she had to nourish herself first. When she slumped forward, too weak to sit, Midas caught her. His wing draped protectively behind her, his chest curved inward like a shield.

Elowen felt like she might have drifted into a light sleep when she felt a warm cloth touch her shaky, clammy skin.

Slowly, silently, Midas cleaned the dried blood and afterbirth from her thighs, her calves, the raw curve of her hips. He worked delicately like he feared she might shatter beneath him. His tail moved behind him in slow, soothing arcs, a silent lullaby meant only for her.

She winced once, her body tender, and Midas stilled immediately.

"I am sorry you hurt," he whispered. A truth. A sorrow.

She didn't respond, too drained to form words. Instead,

she leaned against him, letting his heat cradle her while her children fed.

He inhaled the scent of her—blood and milk and life—and closed his eyes. She had given him everything. And what could he offer in return? Gold? Gems? No. She deserved more than that.

She deserved *worship*.

His hands, still too large and clawed, trembled as they stroked her back. He whispered dragon-words into her hair. Old things. Sacred things. "You," he said, voice low and hoarse, "are...mine."

But not as hoard. Not as prize. As *beloved*. As *precious*.

The twins mewled softly between them. One hiccuped. The other clung to Elowen's breast with small fingers.

Midas looked down at them, and for a moment, his vision blurred with heat and wetness he couldn't recognize.

THE FIRE CRACKLED SOFTLY against the stone walls of the cave, casting long, flickering shadows that danced across the hoard of treasures nestled deep in the far corners. Elowen lay propped on a thick bed of blankets and woven pelts, her body still aching but no longer trembling. Midas had not left her side. Even now, he sat close, his legs crossed awkwardly beneath him in his humanoid form, tail coiled gently behind him, wings folded like a blanket at his back. His hand hovered near her thigh, not quite touching, but always near.

Nestled between them lay the boys, bundled in soft cloths made from a stolen priest's robe and a weathered tapestry Midas had long ago hidden beneath gold. The infants were quiet now, their bellies full, their tiny fingers twitching in their sleep.

They looked like her. But also like him. They had her mouth, her nose, but their eyes...those golden eyes were Midas', down to the molten ring around the iris.

Elowen's voice broke the silence, hushed and reverent.

"They need names."

Midas turned to look at her, head tilting ever so slightly. "Names." He blinked slowly. Her heart warmed at that. He still spoke in short sentences, his tongue wrapping clumsily around human words. But his meaning was never unclear.

"These are our miracles," she said. "Their names will be written into history."

Midas looked down at the boys, his gaze almost painfully tender. "You choose."

Elowen's lips parted. "Me?"

He nodded once. "You carried them. Brought them here. To name offspring is an honor only mother dragons carry. A tradition we shall keep."

She looked down at the first boy. He shifted in his sleep and let out a tiny grunt.

"Kalen," she whispered. "It means light."

Midas repeated the word slowly, tasting it in the back of his throat. "Kalen."

His voice was rich with approval. She turned to the second, the smaller of the two. He slept without sound, his mouth slightly open.

"Auric," she said, softer this time. "It means golden. Fitting, I think."

A flicker of something bright crossed Midas' face. "Kalen. Auric."

He repeated their names as though they were ancient spells. His tail curled around all three of them in a loose, protective circle.

Elowen smiled, even through the soreness, even through the fading aches in her limbs.

"Kalen and Auric," she whispered again, her eyes glassy with unshed tears. "Our boys."

Midas leaned closer. With a clawed hand far gentler than it had any right to be, he traced a line between her shoulder and neck—a silent expression of awe. "Ours."

He said it like a vow. Like a prayer. Elowen exhaled shakily, her gaze flickering between the newborns, her dragon, and the fire.

THIRTY-TWO

Midas had never been afraid of his own strength.

Not in war. Not in hunger. Not when he roared loud enough to shake the snow from mountaintops or snapped an ancient oak with a swipe of his tail.

But now, the ancient, powerful beast that he was, trembled at the sound of his sons breathing.

They were *so small*. Frail and soft, with fluttering hearts and paper-thin cries. Their hands were barely bigger than the tip of his claw, their bones light as dry leaves. When they lay beside Elowen's chest, curling into her warmth, they looked like nothing more than petals.

Petals he could crush without meaning to.

He stayed at the mouth of the cave. Watching. Waiting. *Protecting*. But never close enough to touch.

Elowen had asked him once, "*Would you like to hold them?*"

He had stared at her. Panicked. Then looked at his human-shaped hands. *What if he dropped them? What if his talons snagged their skin? What if his fire, ancient and deep as magma, was too much for their delicate bodies?*

So he had shaken his head, though the pain of that decision weighed on him every day.

Instead, he watched them sleep from the shadows. Watched as one curled his tiny hand around her finger. Watched the other stir and coo softly in dreams. Elowen sang to them in a voice so soft it felt like prayer. When she looked over at Midas, she smiled.

"You don't have to be afraid of them," she said one night, her voice gentle.

But she didn't understand. It wasn't them he feared. It was *himself.*

"You are their father, Midas," she pressed. "I trust you. You won't hurt them."

Still, he could not bring himself to risk it yet. He shifted back into his natural form to avoid the conversation, and kept a distance from the three of them until she fell asleep. The twins were nestled between her arms, one resting just beneath her chin, the other splayed like a starfish across her stomach.

Midas crept closer, each step slow and deliberate. He folded his wings in tight. Tucked his claws beneath him. Lowered his head to the cool stone floor.

Close enough now that he could hear their breath, two soft rhythms that beat in sync. He watched the rise and fall of their chests. Watched the way they kicked in their dreams. One gave a soft snort and made a sound he'd never heard before—*a laugh.*

Something clutched at his chest. He lowered his snout

just enough to feel the brush of warmth from their small bodies.

And then a tiny hand came reaching aimlessly, landing with a soft pat between his nostrils. Midas froze. His son didn't even open his eyes before he giggled sleepily and went still again.

Elowen stirred.

"Midas?" she whispered groggily. He rumbled back a response, just loud enough for her to know he was there.

She fell still with sleep again in an instant, and it warmed his heart. She trusted him enough with their children to fall asleep so easily, knowing he was so close.

He lay there the rest of the night, head beside his greatest treasures, learning what it meant to be strong in a way that was reserved not for the world, but for his family.

ELOWEN SAT on a blanket of fur, twin bundles nestled against her chest. One stirred, a tiny hand stretching open with a soundless yawn before curling again. The other smacked his lips in sleep, a droplet of drool collecting on Elowen's shoulder.

Midas stood a few paces away. He had taken his human form, the shift leaving his body trembling from the strain. He said nothing. He only stared, eyes wide and molten as they fixed on his perfect sons.

Elowen reached up and brushed a strand of hair from her

brow, her body still exhausted from the toll of birth, but radiant in the firelight. "Come here," she said gently. "You need to hold them, my heart. Come embrace what we created together."

Midas didn't move at first.

"What if I hurt them?" he whispered painfully, as if it had already happened.

"No," Elowen murmured. "You never could."

With painstaking care, she lifted the larger of the twins —Kalen—and extended him out in her arms. Midas approached like one would step in a temple, every step heavy with awe. He knelt before her, eyes flicking between Elowen's steady hands and the tiny creature she carried.

Kalen stirred as he was passed over, his small brow furrowing, lips pressing together in protest. Midas took him with hands that trembled, fingers curled protectively beneath his son's back and head. The warmth of the boy's body shocked him. The heartbeat, even more.

So fragile. So real.

Midas bowed his head over the small figure and inhaled deeply. Kalen smelled of his mother's milk, of warmth, of something ancient and nearly forgotten.

Elowen watched from the nest with the other boy in her arms, quietly watching and forcing her expression to stay steady for him. Midas pressed a kiss to the top of Kalen's head as she handed him Auric next.

This one stirred immediately in his father's arms, letting out a squeaky whimper. Midas exhaled a shuddering breath and pulled both twins to his chest, one in each arm, cradled with care that was becoming of the most delicate treasures in his hoard.

He knelt there for a long time. The silence was thick

with emotion. It stretched and shimmered around them like spun gold. When Midas finally looked up, tears streaked his cheeks.

"They are dragons," he whispered, awed. He turned his head to look at Elowen, as if he were seeing her anew. "You gave them to me," he said, almost in disbelief. "You gave me a future."

Elowen reached forward and pressed her forehead to his, their sons between them. "You gave me a home first."

He nodded once, fiercely, as if that meant more to him than anything else in the world.

It did.

IT HAD TAKEN weeks before the toll of birth had finally passed through Elowen's body. She appeared brighter and had more energy than before, but she was still tired. So very tired. Her sons took up all of her attention and time.

Midas had done his best to tend to her while her body recovered. It had taken weeks—but now he knew in the soft exhale of sleep that true rest claimed her.

She needed sleep. She *deserved* sleep. And this morning, at last, she had found it, and he would not be the one to take it from her.

The twins were already stirring, wriggling in their woven basket beside the hearth, their soft cries just beginning to rise.

Midas moved quietly. He quickly learned to cradle them

in his human arms, though the awkwardness still lingered in his joints and fingers. His claws followed him in this form, and the fear of their sharpness haunted his grip, making him overly cautious.

He gathered the boys to his chest and padded barefoot across the cave's smooth stone to the small copper basin Elowen used for washing. He had filled it earlier, fetching water from the river and warming it with stones heated with his own breath.

He placed them gently into the shallow water. The boys kicked their legs, one smacking the water with an eager splash.

Midas flinched. But they laughed. The sound was *music.* Something he was not expecting to hear so soon after their birth. He chuckled softly under his breath, ears twitching as he reached for the washcloth.

You are loud, he murmured to them in dragon tongue, voice gravel-thick and low. *Louder than thunder.*

One of them hiccupped and gurgled in reply as if they understood him.

Yes, you, he teased.

He worked slowly, carefully wiping between the creases of their tiny limbs, washing behind their ears the way Elowen always did. He whispered nonsense in the language of dragons, stringing together old tales, half-remembered legends from before the fall.

There was once a dragon who could speak to the moon, he told them, dipping the cloth again. *She sang silver songs, soft as snow, into the beauty of the night...*

He rinsed them gently, using his cupped hand to pour water over their bellies. One kicked again, this time catching Midas' forearm with more force than expected, causing a smile to creep to his face.

Good. You will be strong, he growled affectionately. *Like your mother.*

Elowen stirred. From the bed of furs and moss they shared, she blinked against the morning light, her eyes searching instinctively for her children. But the sight that greeted her instead stilled her breath.

There, by the fire, Midas sat human-shaped—his long, unkempt hair falling in strands around his face, wings curled loosely behind him. He was hunched over the copper basin, the twins nestled safely in his lap, both freshly clean and blinking at their father as he spoke softly in a tongue she could not understand.

For the first time since the twins were born, her body felt light. Her heart felt quiet. She wasn't needed in that moment—not as a healer, or a protector, or a mother scrambling to stay ahead of exhaustion.

Midas had the boys, and they were *safe.*

I think the moon dragon was very lonely, he murmured to the twins, cupping a hand around the back of one small neck. *I think she sang because she was waiting for something.* Midas lowered his head, brushing his brow against the tops of their hair. His breath caught in his throat as he whispered:

I understood that sorrow. But no longer.

Elowen sat propped against the wall of furs, a thick blanket draped around her shoulders, her eyes fluttering closed for just a moment before snapping open again. Midas had brought the boys to her side after turning to find her awake. They were nestled beside her, swaddled and content after nursing, their small hands curled into fists like budding flower petals.

She was always watching them. Always reaching for them, checking their warmth, smoothing their hair, whispering soft assurances even when they could barely hear.

Though he admired her devotion, it troubled Midas how quickly she forgot herself. How often she forgot to eat. To rest. So today, he brought the food to her.

Roasted root vegetables mixed with soft greens and the meat he'd hunted the day before, carefully shredded and cooked to her liking. It wasn't perfect—he still didn't fully grasp the balance of flavors—but it was warm. He presented it to her on a carved wooden bowl, waiting with unblinking patience until she looked up.

"Eat," he said softly, still learning how to shape the words in her tongue with confidence.

Elowen smiled sleepily, but obediently took the dish. "Thank you."

Midas didn't sit far. He hovered like a shadow, just within reach, eyes flicking between her and the twins as she ate. He relaxed only when he saw her take the second bite without hesitation.

"Always looking at *them*," he said after a moment, his tone more observation than complaint. She glanced down at the boys, who slept curled together. "You are everything to them. Warmth. Safety. Nourishment. But they need you strong."

He watched her chew slowly, her fingers trembling just slightly from fatigue she hadn't admitted aloud. Then her gaze lifted, softer now. Thoughtful.

"Midas..." she began, her voice hesitant, "do you think

they'll always look like this? Like *me*?" He tilted his head curiously. "They have your eyes," she murmured, "but sometimes I wonder...will they grow wings? Horns? Tails? Will they shift?"

Midas looked to the boys again. "I do not know," he said carefully. "But I have imagined it."

Her brow lifted gently. "Imagined?"

His golden eyes flickered like embers. "To fly with them," he said. "To hear them roar. Teach them the path of the sky. Teach them fire. The hunt. To be dragon."

There was something wistful in his tone, aching deeply in his chest. Elowen placed the bowl aside, food half-finished now, and reached over to touch his hand. Her fingers laced with his—rough palm to soft skin.

"What if they don't?" she asked, eyes searching his face. "What if they are human like me?"

"They are mine. I love them as they are."

The boys stirred in their sleep, one yawning so wide it made Midas laugh under his breath. He reached out to tuck the fur more securely around them, careful not to wake them.

Elowen leaned against his shoulder, the tension leaving her body inch by inch.

And for a moment there was no pain, no fear, and no suffering. Only a human girl, a dragon, and the two lives they created together, deep in the heart of the mountain.

THIRTY-THREE

AT FIRST, Elowen thought she was imagining things.

The way their clothes grew tighter, how their once-wobbly heads now held steady with uncanny strength. But as she laid the boys down beside one another on the soft pelt-lined floor of the cave, her brow furrowed. Their limbs had lengthened. Their tiny bellies had filled out. They had been born scarcely a full moon ago...and yet, they looked more like human toddlers than newborns.

She brushed a finger down one of their arms, then glanced at Midas, who stood nearby with a haunch of meat balanced on one shoulder. His eyes flicked toward her immediately, and then toward the boys. His steps slowed.

"They've grown," she murmured, not quite a question.

Midas stepped closer, setting the meat aside. He lowered himself to one knee beside her and studied their sons with a narrowed gaze. For a long moment, he said nothing, merely watched them with intense focus. Then he exhaled a soft puff of warm air.

"Yes."

Elowen looked up at him sharply. "You're not worried?"

A slow smile curled across his face, sharp-toothed and gleaming with pride.

"*Dragon*," he said. He reached out and gently touched one of the boys' legs, marveling at the steady kick it gave in return. "Good seed. Good bones. Strong."

Elowen blinked, startled. "You think it's...a *good* thing?"

Midas gave a small, emphatic grunt of agreement. "It means..." he said, tapping a clawed fingertip gently to his temple to find the words. "Fly sooner. Bite harder. Hotter fire." He turned to her, eyes bright with pride. "They are *mine*."

Elowen wasn't sure whether to laugh or cry. The thought of her sons soaring through the skies—*flying, for heaven's sake*—was still almost too much to process when her womb hadn't yet adjusted to the emptiness.

"But they're not even crawling yet," she whispered.

Midas said. "Soon they run. Then I lead them to sky."

He said the last word with such reverence that it caught her breath. She looked at the boys again, at their sharp golden eyes blinking slowly, at the faint flickers of shimmer beneath their skin. She hadn't imagined that either. In the right light, it was there—scattered patches of something like scale beneath their soft baby flesh.

Midas sat beside her now, watching her closely.

"You have fear of this?" he asked, softer.

She hesitated. "I don't know," she admitted. "I just... didn't expect them to grow so quickly. What if it means they'll age faster than humans? Faster than my heart will accept?"

Midas frowned, processing her words. Then, without speaking, he reached out and cupped the back of her head with one large, warm hand, pulling her gently until her temple rested against his chest. His heartbeat was slow and thunderous beneath her cheek.

"Dragons live long. Do not fear time."

Elowen nodded slowly, curling one arm around his side as she closed her eyes. The boys shifted in their sleep, and Midas tucked a fur more securely around them both.

That night, just as Midas and Elowen fell into deep slumber, they were awoken by the shrill, pained cries of their boys.

And the screaming did not stop.

Not at dawn, when the first light touched the mouth of the cave. Not at dusk, when the fire burned low and Midas wrapped his wings tight around the family nest. Not even in the deepest hours of night, when the wind outside howled through the mountain.

Auric wailed until his voice cracked. Kalen thrashed and kicked, sobbing as if something inside him were trying to claw its way out. Their little bodies curled and jerked in spasms neither fever nor injury could explain.

Midas paced in his natural form. Endlessly. His claws left long gouges in the stone. His wings trembled from exhaustion. His eyes, once proud and golden, had dulled into something panicked and hollow. He was a creature built to reduce cities to ash—and he could do *nothing* to stop the cries of his sons.

"I don't know what to do," Elowen whispered, voice hoarse with sleeplessness. "They won't latch, Midas. What is wrong with them?"

She knelt in the nest, one child cradled against each shoulder, her gown stiff with dried blood from where their noses had bled. Both boys were slick with sweat and tears, and neither one responded to soothing words or herbal balm. They clawed at their own skin, their heads, their backs, as if something inside was hurting them.

Unable to shift, Midas stood at the edge of the nest, rigid with fury—*not* at her, never at her—but at his help-lessness. His *uselessness.* He had lived through war, famine, betrayal. But nothing had ever broken him like this.

They're not sick, Midas murmured to himself in the cadence of his language. *Not...wrong.*

Elowen cried softly, nearly in despair. "Why won't it *stop?*"

He didn't answer. Because deep inside, he feared he knew the truth. He had known the time would come. Had *prayed* it would come. But not like this. Not with terror and blood and agony.

It took three nights before it all made sense.

Elowen had drifted into a brief, fitful sleep, one arm looped protectively around Auric's tiny body. Midas sat beside her in dragon form, wings draped like a sheltering canopy, eyes unblinking.

A new scent hit his nose. *Blood.* Fresh. Sharp. He rose, panic gripping his chest. *Had something entered the cave? An intruder?*

But the scent was *here.* Beneath his wing. From *them.*

He bent low. A soft whimper escaped Kalen's lips—and then, as if a dam burst, a scream followed.

Elowen jolted awake, clutching both boys to her. And there, smeared across their bedding of soft furs and woven cloth, was *blood*. It soaked the boys' backs and pooled beneath them.

But neither was crying anymore. They blinked up at her, their small faces dazed but calm, as if the agony had finally passed and a rush of relief had soothed them. She looked down, and her breath caught.

Tiny horns, the same burnished obsidian as their father's, jutted from beneath sweat-matted curls. Still soft, not yet fully grown. And from their shoulder blades emerged the bare beginnings of *wings*.

Not human. *Dragon.*

Elowen clutched a hand to her mouth in pure disbelief. "Midas..." she whispered.

But he was already moving, his massive head bowing down to examine them, to sniff, to touch his snout against the blood-slick horns. His great body shook from something like awe. His children *were* dragons, and not just in name or eye or instinct. In body, in heart, in soul.

He gave a soft, reverent sound. A note from the dragon tongue that Elowen had come to recognize as *'I am pleased'*.

Kalen cooed at the sound like it was the most beautiful thing he had ever heard in his short life. Auric smiled and curled his clawed toes, listening intently to the grumble from his father's throat. And just like that, the world was right again.

Elowen and Midas lay curled on either side of the boys, watching them sleep at last—tucked beneath a blanket despite the blood stains, each twin's tiny wings twitching as they dreamed.

"I suppose you'll be teaching them to fly soon," Elowen

said, brushing the soft horns with a gentle fingertip. Then, her voice broke with the unending love for her family. "Don't let them forget about me while they're reclaiming the skies with you."

THIRTY-FOUR

TUCKED into their nest of blankets and moss, the boys slept like creatures that knew they were capable of ruling the skies.

Elowen watched them for a long time before she rose from the floor, stretching with a soft sound of effort, and padded barefoot across the stone to where Midas lay at the cave's edge in his dragon form—coiled like a question mark, head resting near the fire. She climbed onto his foreleg without a word and settled into the crook of his body, curling against his chest like a second heartbeat.

He shifted, his breath stirring her hair, and wrapped his tail around her like a ribbon. It had become pure instinct, to wrap himself around her and the boys while he rested.

They sat in silence for a while, listening to the hush between the flames and the breaths escaping from their chests.

Then Elowen spoke, voice low and hushed as to not

disturb the children. "Do you ever wonder how we got here?"

Midas blinked one golden eye open. She smiled and continued. "It feels like a story someone else might have told me. A woman and a dragon in a cave and two little miracles." Midas huffed softly, his breath warm against her arm. "I think I would've wanted to believe it. And now that it's real..."

He remained quiet, simply listening to her voice. She reached out and ran her fingers along one of the larger scales at his chest—worn smooth with time, edged in gold. "I never thought I'd have children," she murmured. "When I was in that village, I was too wrong for love, and somehow I began to believe it. That place took too many pieces of myself to ever be whole enough to raise someone else."

Midas tilted his head slightly, listening. "And yet," she continued, "when I see them playing and laughing and growing—I know it was all because of you. You gave me space to believe in beautiful things again."

He swallowed and nudged her affectionately. She looked up at him, meeting his gaze. But she never needed an answer from him, she only wanted him to listen. "You love in your own way," she said, leaning her head against him again. "With warmth. With protection. With every bone in your body. And that's how our boys will love too. I hope that the world will be kinder to them than it was to us."

He was still for a long moment. Then, with a careful shift, he began to return to his human shape—limbs narrowing, wings shrinking, horns curling close to his scalp. When he was fully formed, he wrapped his arms around her and pulled her close. She climbed into his lap without hesitation, straddling his legs, chest against his. He rested his chin on her shoulder, and she buried her face into the curve of his neck.

They stayed like that—breathing each other in.

"I was afraid," he said quietly, his voice slower in this form. "When you were with child. I did not know if I could be...father. Or what that meant. But now I know that they are my greatest blessings. My most valuable treasures." Midas looked at the sleeping twins, their chests rising and falling in tandem. "They are the best thing I have ever done," he said.

She pulled back, cupped his face in her hands. "It's the best thing we've done."

He leaned forward and kissed her forehead, lips warm and slow. Then he moved slowly down her cheek until he reached the tender spot under her ear that he had learned made her shiver. In the hush that followed, Elowen whispered: "Everything is so perfect now. Sometimes I wish time would stop here."

But as she spoke those words, something shifted in the wind, and the breeze carried the scent to Midas.

Smoke. Metal. Man.

He lifted his head from Elowen's neck and gently moved her aside so he could shift once more. His nostrils flared wide and his eyes turned a more wild shade of gold, the pupils dilating for better sight. He used his tail to keep Elowen back as he approached the mouth of the cave, and there, below, barely visible through the mist of the lower cliffs, figures moved among the rocks.

Humans. Armed. Too close.

He was on his feet in a heartbeat, wings flaring wide as a bellow tore from his chest—low, guttural, warning. Elowen touched his tail, her voice faint. "Midas? What is it?"

He didn't answer. Couldn't. He crouched low at the ridge, teeth bared, heart thundering in his chest.

They found us.

His mind spiraled—images flashing behind his eyes like lightning. Elowen screaming in pain. His sons, pink and helpless, blinking up at him with his own golden eyes. Their tiny hands, the weight of them in his claws. The soft curve of Elowen's smile as she whispered their names.

Mine.

A deep growl crawled up his throat like a curse summoned from the depths of the world. The damp rocks beneath his claws began to steam.

The humans drew closer, unaware of what waited above. One of them carried a long weapon—primitive, but deadly enough. Another held a torch.

Fire. Destruction. Screaming. He remembered his kin falling. Remembered mothers screaming as their young were slaughtered in nests. Remembered how men cheered when dragons died.

Midas leapt out of the cave mouth without warning. The wind cracked around him as he dove, wings slicing the air like blades. His roar shattered the stillness of the mountain, echoing like the voice of a god long forgotten. Below, the men froze, one stumbling backward in terror.

Midas didn't care.

He hit the ground like a meteor, talons driving into the earth. The ground exploded around him in a wave of heat as he inhaled deep and let his fury out in a pillar of fire. The torch-bearer screamed. His flame licked the rocks, the trees, the bones of the earth. They ran.

Cowards! Insects!

One fell, stumbling over their own useless feet. Midas was on him in an instant, jaws snapping shut just inches from the man's leg. He didn't kill him. Not *yet*. He wanted him terrified, so that when they returned to their stinking villages they would speak of the beast who was no longer afraid of the humans. Midas wanted him to see what awaited those who dared threaten his den.

He lifted his head and let out a second roar, louder than the first, a sound so ancient and furious it made birds scatter from the cliffs.

Then he turned his fire on the path they'd climbed.

Flame poured from his mouth in waves, searing stone, destroying every foothold and ledge. The mountain itself seemed to groan beneath the heat. No path would remain. No trail.

He scorched it all.

When he returned to the cave, his scales still glowed faintly with heat. Elowen was waiting for him just inside, holding the boys to her chest, crying and trembling from being awakened by the noise. Her face was pale, eyes wide. He stepped close and pressed his head gently to her side, careful of the children.

He growled low, wings curling forward as if to wrap them all in armor. She rested her hand against his jaw. "We are safe," she murmured, hoping it would bring some peace to his fury. She had never seen him so fearsome, not even when they whipped her against the post.

He lowered himself to the floor, coiling around her and the twins like a wall of living stone. His breathing was heavy. His heart raced. He kept his keen eyes on the cave mouth, daring anything to approach.

A whisper burned in his chest, ancient and instinctual: *Mine. Mine. Mine.*

When the boys finally settled once more, Elowen sat on the edge of their bed of furs, one of the twins nestled against her chest, the other asleep beside her. The cave was quiet now, save for the crackle of the fire and the distant hiss of wind against stone. But the quiet did little to slow her heart.

She had seen Midas furious before but never quite like this. Not the type of fury that lingered long after the danger left. Never with that sharpness he could not seem to soften. The type of fury that turned the very air hot and left scorched earth in its wake.

She had held her sons tighter when he returned, glowing from within like a star barely cooled. She knew he'd never harm them—but some ancient part of her, the human part, had recoiled at the sheer power he wielded. She hadn't said anything about it, but he had noticed anyway.

Now he stood before her human-shaped, half-shadowed by the firelight.

His chest rose and fell with slow, deliberate breath. His skin was streaked with onyx and gold, scaled faintly at the ribs. His wings were folded tightly behind his back, still heavy with tension. His horns curved backward like a crown, catching the firelight with every breath. And his eyes—still gold and molten—never left her face.

"I scared you." His voice was deeper in this form, but quieter. He said the words as a statement, not a question. Elowen didn't answer immediately. She adjusted the boy in her arms, gently swaying. He lowered his head. His hands curled into fists at his sides. "I would never hurt them. Or you."

"I know," she said. But her voice was too soft, and she was still trembling.

Midas stepped forward, slower now. He knelt before her on the stone floor—almost as tall as her even like this, but subdued. Subservient. His wings drooped slightly, tail curled close to his body. "I was not angry at you," he said. "Or them."

"I know," she repeated.

"I only saw the danger. I smelled their fire, their steel." His jaw tensed, voice shaking slightly. "I saw the old world again. The one that killed my kind. The one that would kill you for loving me. The world that would rip our boys from your arms without a second thought." His eyes flicked to the twins, their tiny chests rising and falling. "I would burn the sky, the moon, and the stars before I let them touch you. I am fire. I know this," he said, voice raw. "But I will never turn it on you. I did not mean to frighten you. I only know one way to keep you safe. And I would never hesitate to do it."

A long pause stretched between them. Elowen reached out and touched the base of one of his horns. Her fingers traced the curve gently, like she was reassuring herself he was real.

"You don't have to explain, Midas," she said at last. "I

just…I suppose in our bliss I forgot that the gentle dragon I fell in love with would burn the world for me."

He exhaled shakily and pressed his forehead to her knee. The gesture, so animalistic, yet so human in its humility—broke something in her.

She leaned forward, cradling his face in one hand, her other arm still wrapped around their son, and the weight of the reality she had forgotten resting between them like mirror that had begun to fracture.

THIRTY-FIVE

THE LAKE STRETCHED WIDE and still beneath the afternoon sun, its surface glittering with ripples like threads of silk. Warmth pressed down gently from above, golden and slow-moving, and the air buzzed faintly with the hum of bees and the flutter of insect wings.

They were alone here, tucked into a meadow where the grass grew tall and the world forgot to look, in the sacred place where the fires of Elowen and Midas' love had first been tempered.

Elowen lay back on a woven blanket, her hair spread like silk against the soft earth, her dress wrinkled and sun-warmed. Her head was turned slightly to the side, eyes half-lidded, watching the children.

The twins toddled a few feet away in the grass, round and soft with the plumpness of toddlerhood. One was chasing a pale-winged butterfly, arms outstretched in clumsy wonder. The other had fallen onto his bottom and was laughing at the way the wind lifted dandelion fluff into the air.

Midas sat behind Elowen, his legs stretched out long in front of him, his wings and tail relaxed. His human form glowed faintly in the light, skin kissed with gold, his dark hair tousled by the breeze, one braid that Elowen had woven with locks of her own falling from right above his ear. One arm was braced on the ground behind him; the other forearm rested over his bent knee.

But it was his tail that united them all. It had curled around them in a loose circle. A border. A wall of warm, scaled flesh that enclosed them in the softest kind of protection.

One of the boys tripped, and Elowen sat up instantly, but Midas was faster—his tail caught the child with a gentle thud, nudging him upright again before he could cry. The boy blinked, wide-eyed, then giggled and stumbled back toward his brother.

Elowen exhaled a breath of quiet relief and settled back on her elbows. Midas didn't speak. He didn't need to. He only watched her and the way the sunlight touched her cheekbones. The way she tilted her head when one of the boys shrieked in delight. The way her eyes softened when she looked at them—like the very sight of their children smoothed the raw edges of the world.

She wasn't smiling for him. She didn't know he was watching. And that made it all the more precious.

And he saw, with perfect clarity, something he hadn't dared to acknowledge fully before—not until this very moment. Elowen had never pitied him. Nor did she tolerate him out of necessity or loneliness. She had never looked at him as something to fix, or to endure. From the very beginning, she had looked at him and *chosen* him.

He, who was made of fire. He, who had lost his kind and carried that rage in his bones. And still she had loved him. Had trusted him with her life. Her body. Her children.

Midas' chest ached with something soft and too large to name. He leaned forward and pressed a kiss to her temple, his breath warm against her skin. He hummed low in his throat at her comforting scent and nuzzled against her gently, pulling the curl of his tail in closer.

The children laughed again, chasing nothing in particular, whole lives ahead of them. They had no reason to expect violence. Not today.

Which was why it came like a knife to the back.

The first arrow struck the water with a wet thunk. The second embedded itself in a tree just behind Elowen's head. She turned—and froze.

There were six men from the village. It was the same men that threatened his den from before—he could smell them. Dirty, red-faced, their eyes wild with fear and righteous hatred. And in their hands—swords. Ropes. Torches. Tools of destruction.

"Get the demon children!" one shouted. "Before they grow fangs and burn the rest of us!"

Elowen screamed. Midas was already moving—body convulsing, the sound of bones shifting, magic flaring like lightning through the air. His skin split, wings tearing forth, horns curling into place as his form ballooned into shadow and gold and death.

But they were so close. There was no time to think.

Elowen scooped the twins into her arms, one under each arm, their little faces panicked, mouths open in confusion.

She bolted into the trees, trusting Midas to find them where they would hide, branches whipping against her arms, her feet raw and bloodied on the forest floor. Behind her, she heard Midas roar in the way that could crack mountains down the middle and end cities in a breath.

The men had scattered, the stronger ones acting as a distraction for Midas, the others following her. They caught her less than a mile into the trees.

One man tackled her from behind, sending the twins tumbling to the dirt. Elowen fought—biting, clawing, screaming. But they tore her away. Two more men pinned her down, pressing her face into the leaves.

"Hold her. Make her watch."

Kalen screamed, arms flailing in her direction. His brother just cried, reaching for her. They pinned the children, too.

"No—no, no please!" Elowen sobbed, voice breaking. "They're children. They haven't done anything! Do whatever you want to me, just please don't hurt them!"

"Dragon spawn," spat the man with the knife. "We won't let them grow into monsters!"

He turned the blade in his hand. And then there was a scream.

It wasn't Elowen's. It was Kalen's. A high, raw, baby's scream. They had cut off one of his horns without mercy or remorse. Blood gushed over his face, his sobs hiccupping into something soundless. His twin shrieked, trying to get to him.

Elowen howled, pulling against her restraints with

everything she had. Her wrists tore, her back split open again where a whip cracked down. Once. Twice.

"Stop it!" she screamed. "Please stop! I'll do anything—just stop hurting them!"

"Cut out her cursed womb!" one of them said. "We must burn it! Purge the world of its evil!"

None of them saw the shadow pass overhead. Not the men. Not Elowen. Not the boys.

They only heard the sound; the sudden silence of the forest, as if the trees themselves had gasped.

Midas landed so hard trees were ripped from their roots from the force. He did not roar this time. He didn't need to.

The first man was crushed before he could draw another breath. The second was impaled with talons larger than his body. The third tried to run but made it only two steps before Midas' tail lashed out and snapped his spine like dry wood.

The one that held Kalen's severed horn like a trophy turned, dagger raised, and Midas opened his jaws.

Flame made of raw rage escaped his throat. It scorched the earth, reduced the trees to ash, superheated the air until the man ceased to exist—not even ashes remained.

Midas stood heaving, breath ragged, smoke rising from the trees around them. His claws were soaked with blood. His wings were trembling with adrenaline and wrath.

And then his eyes fell on Elowen.

She was still tied down with ropes, struggling with panic to break free. She was bleeding and bruised. Midas used his great claws to slice through the ropes, and Elowen instantly scooped her children to her chest, hovering over them like a shield.

Her boys lay on the ground under her, scared and crying —Kalen limp with pain. Midas made a sound then, deep and guttural, an animal's cry of grief. He stepped forward and lowered his head. He gathered Elowen, then the boys—cradled them all.

He carried them back to the cave in silence.

WHEN HE LANDED at the mouth of the cave, Midas moved deeper and laid them down gently.

Elowen first, nestled against the soft bed of furs. She hadn't spoken once since he'd untied her, not even when her feet bled or her arms shook so badly she nearly dropped the children. Her eyes had been glassy, far away, and her breath was shallow and quick, caught high in her chest. She did not respond to his voice. She did not respond when her sons whimpered for her. Her hands fluttered once, then fell still.

Her lashes trembled, and then her body collapsed entirely, her breath caught in a half-sob before silence overtook her. Midas froze.

Elowen? he asked, voice thick with fear. No answer.

He shifted down into his human form, barely breathing through the pain of it. He knelt beside her and pressed a hand to her cheek. Her skin was clammy. Pale. Her body too limp. Too still. The attack had sent her into a panic, and she had gone someplace inside herself that he could not reach.

For a moment, terror gripped him in a way even the

death of his kind never had. This was a wound no salve could heal.

He reached for the bowl of springwater they kept near the hearth and soaked a strip of linen in it. Gently he dabbed her forehead, her temples, her wrists. He bundled her close with another fur, wrapping her trembling body as one might swaddle a wounded bird.

"You are safe," he whispered, over and over again, though he wasn't sure if it was for her sake or his.

He turned next to the twins. Auric was curled into a ball, hiccuping small cries into his fists. Midas touched his back and murmured in dragon-tongue, the words sacred and old, made of warmth and earth and firelight. Slowly, Auric shifted closer to his father, burying himself in the crook of Midas' folded legs.

Kalen whimpered, still bleeding, his tiny hands twitching with pain. Midas bent over him like a prayer. He wrapped the child's head with a cloth soaked in salve—Elowen's teachings serving him well now.

He remembered her teaching him which blend soothed pain, which one sealed wounds. His fingers were too big for such delicate work, but he forced himself to be careful. He worked with trembling, reverent hands, coating Kalen's wound with the salves mixed together.

It was like caring for embers; one breath too harsh and they might go out.

When Kalen's bandages were secured, Midas lifted both boys into his arms. He sat with them cradled against his chest, Elowen beside him, unmoving but breathing now—slow and steady. He rocked his sons gently, his voice humming again in that ancient cadence only dragons remembered.

His lullaby was low and melodic, a song of caves and fire and hoarded love.

But inside his heart, Midas felt that bitter agony of failure, and would never forgive himself.

THIRTY-SIX

THE CAVE WAS silent but for the breath of the fire and the soft, choked sounds of the twins crying in their sleep.

Elowen lay between them, one arm curled protectively around Kalen, whose bandaged head rested on her chest. His small face was blotchy, cheeks wet with salt and blood. His twin clutched at her other side like he no longer trusted the world.

She hadn't spoken much since the forest. Her voice was cracked, her throat too raw. Her wrists were bruised, her back bloodied again. But her body was still here, and so were her sons.

Midas had not left their side. He'd returned to his smaller human form and sat motionless on the stone floor, just beyond their nest of furs. His hands were clenched tightly in his lap, as though he didn't trust himself to touch them.

Elowen stirred.

Her head turned toward him. Her voice was nothing but

a whisper. "They hurt my boys." He looked at her then, eyes bright with molten gold scorching beneath the surface. "They took his horn," she said, her voice ready to weep again.

Midas moved closer, watching her gently trace patterns on Kalen's tender brow. She didn't flinch when Midas reached out—only leaned into the hand he placed on her shoulder. He was steady and warm against the frigid chill of fear and anger in her veins. She closed her eyes and exhaled through cracked lips.

"I didn't know people could be that cruel to children," she murmured.

"I did," Midas said.

She stared at him for a long moment. "Is this what they did to your siblings?"

Midas nodded. "Our horns were their trophies. Some humans still wear them around their necks like jewelry."

Elowen shuddered at that, her mind racing with the thought that her own kind would slaughter her children and wear their bones around their necks.

Midas placed his hand on her back, fingers feather-light, brushing over the welts there, raised over healed flesh from the last time they whipped her. She didn't react, her mind and body too lost in concern for her son to register the pain.

Elowen ran her fingers gently over Kalen's hair, avoiding the fresh bandage across his temple. She hadn't looked beneath it since Midas applied the salve and wrapped it. She couldn't. She was not ready to see what they had done to him.

She held him tighter. And finally, the words broke loose

from her throat—shaky and breathless and soaked in guilt and rage.

"They didn't do it because they were afraid." Her voice cracked on the last word. Midas lifted his head slowly. She looked down at her son's bruised cheek, her tears falling soundlessly onto his curls. "They didn't cut his horn to protect themselves. They didn't think it would stop him from becoming like you. They just...wanted him to suffer."

Midas said nothing. He didn't need to. She could feel the tension rolling off him like smoke. But she couldn't stop. The words kept coming, hot and shaking.

"I should've stopped them. I should've fought harder. I should've let them kill me before they touched him." Her body began to shake. "I couldn't move—I couldn't save him —" She bent over, folding protectively over Kalen's small body, sobbing silently. "I let them hurt our baby."

Midas finally moved. He closed the space between them and held her to his chest much in the same way she cradled Kalen. His long tail curled around them all.

"I flew so fast I tore the wind apart, but too slow to stop his suffering." His gaze went to the children, his breath shallow. "I failed to protect. It is what I was made for but when they needed me, I wasn't there. They knew it would not grow back. They knew it would mark him. They knew it would remind us how cruel they are." Elowen flinched, her hand pressing over Kalen's curls again. "They wanted him to feel the missing bone, to feel shame for how he was born." Midas' voice trembled. "That is not justified fear. That is evil."

Elowen whispered, "Will he remember it? The pain?"

"Yes."

She swallowed hard.

"But not just that," Midas said. "He will remember that you held him. That I came. That he is ours. That he survived."

Her lips trembled.

"You gave him love," Midas said. "I gave him fire. They may take his horns, but the world cannot take those things away from him."

"I want to kill them," Elowen whispered suddenly, shaking. "I want to tear them apart."

"You will not have to," Midas said, softly. "Watch over our boys. Rest. When you wake, there will be nothing to fear."

MIDAS LEFT JUST BEFORE DAWN. The air was still. The stars beginning to fade into the violet-blue veil of morning.

When he reached the edge of Elowen's old village, he did not speak. He did not land. He did not offer warnings. He simply flew over the gates and unfolded his fury on a village he should have wiped out the day he rescued Elowen from them. His wings tore through the sky like the unfurling of judgment. His roar cracked the hills. Doors slammed open, and people screamed.

He came down like the ancient God of Flame, claws slicing through wood and bone alike. Fire bled from his mouth in torrents, licking across rooftops, sweeping through crops, searing flesh from fleeing bodies.

He spared no one. Not the men, not the women, not the children.

They burned. They all burned. And by the time the sun crested over the trees, the village was gone; reduced to ash. Buried. Erased.

Midas did not linger to revel in the carnage, for there was nothing left to see but scorched grass and crumbled stones.

He returned to his den before his family woke, his wings black with soot. His claws stained dark. But his eyes were soft again the moment they saw Elowen and his children.

She stirred as he entered the cave, blinking awake, her body still aching and raw. Her eyes flickered to the evidence on his wings and claws, but she did not speak. She knew what he had done, felt it in her bones.

And she was *proud*.

THIRTY-SEVEN

ONE MOON LATER

The twins were fighting again.

They had been increasingly restless. Their play had turned rough and their sleep turned fitful and short. They growled, low and angry when things startled them. They flashed teeth at their mother. When Midas approached, tiny embers of fire flared from their mouths, and smoke curled from their noses when they didn't get their way.

It was getting harder to soothe them. Impossible, even. Kalen, the stronger and larger of the two, lashed out quickly and often, especially when Elowen tried to tend to his scarred horn.

They had grown quickly after the attack at the lake, the fear forcing them to develop quicker. Kalen often snapped when Elowen asked to see his wound, and Auric would often stand between them as if their mother would bring more harm.

"Don't touch me!" he'd scream, throwing the salve across the cave, breaking the clay jar against the stone wall. When Auric turned to comfort him, he'd push back, yelling at his twin: "Leave me alone! Your horns are still there!"

Elowen had lost all of her patience with them, and took a moment to breathe at the mouth of the cave. It was agony, to be unable to help her sons. It was frustrating that they denied her comforts when they used to seek them so often.

Midas' attempts were no better. He approached the twins in his half-shifted form—humanoid with his horns and tail still visible.

He didn't raise his voice, but the boys quieted under his gaze instinctually.

"Kalen," Midas said gently, crouching to meet his eyes. "We are just trying to help you."

"Mama doesn't get it!" Kalen snapped. "You don't get it!"

Midas tilted his head, voice still soft. "Then tell me."

Kalen's fists clenched. His breath was already smoking. "They took my horn because of you!" Midas stilled, but the words kept coming. "I hate it. I hate being like you. We're monsters! That's why they did it!"

"Kalen," Midas said, more quietly now, hiding the hurt in his chest.

"I didn't ask to be like you!" Kalen's voice cracked. "Why couldn't we just be normal?"

Midas couldn't stop himself from stumbling when Kalen shoved him in the chest. The push was nothing. Barely a flicker of weight. But the intent behind it was what hollowed him out and knocked him over.

"You should've let us be human like mama," Kalen

whispered, tears brimming in his eyes. "Then they wouldn't have hurt me."

He turned and ran deeper into the cave. His twin didn't follow. He just stared at their father, eyes wide with second-hand hurt.

Midas remained on his knees for a long moment. And then he rose, turned, and walked out of the cave to stand with Elowen.

She wasn't far, just at the edge of the cliff that had deep groves etched into the stone from years of Midas landing there. Elowen sat silently with her legs dangling over the edge. If she heard what Kalen said, she did not acknowledge it.

Midas shifted into his dragon form and curled tightly into himself. He tried to make himself small and invisible despite being something so large. In his solace of this form, he felt his heart crumble.

He had expected fear from his children, and maybe even confusion. Even anger he could understand.

But rejection? Midas never knew hurt like experiencing that from them.

Though they were his greatest treasures, Midas worried they would never forgive him for making them dragons. It was no longer a source of pride for them—they saw their father the way the rest of the world did: as a monster.

And that hollowed Midas out with guilt and grief nearly too heavy to bear. He would not tell Elowen this, for he did not want her to carry this weight too.

THE DAYS GREW LONGER, and another moon passed.

The boys healed, slowly. Kalen's wound was scabbed and fading into a hard, angry scar. They still played. Still laughed. But never when Midas was close.

And never *with* him.

Elowen noticed it first in the way they began to follow her everywhere. Even more than before. If she went to fetch water, they came. If she tended the garden of delicate herbs by the cliff's edge, they trailed behind her like shadows.

They slept curled around her now, both pressed into her sides, their little hands clinging to her nightdress long after dreams took them.

Midas stopped joining the bedtime nest. He did not want to disturb his children by being so close when they were vulnerable with sleep. Instead, he lay near the cave's mouth in dragon form, his wings folded tight and unmoving, golden eyes open well into the night.

Once, when Elowen stirred before dawn, she found him staring at her, curled with their children, longing in his eyes to be included again. She rose and walked to him silently, laying a hand against his side.

"They don't mean it," she said.

His answer was a quiet, earth-deep rumble of disagreement.

She sat beside him, curling her legs beneath her.

"They're children. They're angry. They don't know where to put it."

It was untrue, and they both knew it. They saw the way Kalen's fear had hardened into suspicion. The way he stared when Midas entered the cave—tense, unmoving, like prey waiting to bolt. The glares. The silence. Once, Kalen even stepped between Midas and Elowen when the former approached—arms out, small and shaking.

The part Elowen couldn't forget was that Midas did not come closer after that, he simply turned away as if he believed he was truly a danger to them.

Now, sitting beside him, Elowen reached for his chest in the dark. "They need time. They are afraid of pain, Midas, not of you."

He turned his head slightly, his horns catching the dim firelight. In the dragon tongue she could not understand, he admitted his greatest grief:

They will grow into fierce dragons and still fear the dragon who raised them.

THIRTY-EIGHT

MIDAS LEARNED what it meant to make himself scarce around his children.

He timed his movements so he passed through the cave when the twins were asleep. He waited until the boys were well out of sight before shifting forms, careful not to startle them with the painful sounds that came with it. It was in the way he kept his voice low when he spoke to Elowen, even when the ache in his chest threatened to crack him open.

From the far edge of the cave, half-hidden behind a column of stone, he observed his sons as one might observe a fresh wound that refused to heal.

Kalen paced more than he used to. His movements were sharp, restless, as if he no longer understood what it meant to exist in his own body. When frustration struck, it struck fast. His growls came more than his laughter now, rising from his chest without warning, smoke feathering at his lips before he even realized he was angry.

Auric, by contrast, had gone quiet. He watched every-thing. Measured it. When Kalen lashed out, Auric moved first—always standing between his brother and the world that scarred him.

And both of them together always seemed to glance toward Midas with an uncertain gaze that broke him in half every time he caught them looking.

They also seemed to both be growing into their dragon forms quicker, if it were even possible. A trauma response—the desire to grow in order to protect themselves and each other better.

Elowen noticed the way their bodies warmed unnaturally when they slept, causing her to break out in an uncomfortable sweat almost every night. There was also a faint glow that sometimes pulsed in their throats when they were upset. Their eyes had begun to turn more draconic, and the circular pupils narrowed into vertical and sharp lines when they wrestled each other.

Midas could feel their dragon blood stirring—old instincts surfacing too early. Fear had curdled into anger and pain sharpened into blame.

At night, when the cave was quiet and the boys slept tangled around Elowen, Midas lay awake at the mouth of the den, wings folded tight, tail wrapped around his own body like a restraint.

He remembered being young like them, where those same feelings had plagued his heart after the fall of the dragons, developing into fire without guidance or context. There was a time, when he was their age, where the fire in his throat had not yet learned cruelty and suffering and survival.

No one had been there to teach him what to do with the rage. No one had told him how to control it.

Midas had wanted to be better for his sons. Wanted to be the kind of father who could *guide* them with the fire instead of letting it act solely as a means of protection like it did for him.

But now Kalen and Auric were so afraid of pain that their entire worldview had been shifted from a single instance of Midas' failure.

Now, his own children saw the dragons through the same lens the world always had: monsters that would be punished for existing.

And if the world had taken his son's horn, their innocence, their sense of safety—then surely it was his fault for bringing them into it at all.

One evening, when Elowen had taken the boys further back into the cave, where the washbasin rested to wash their hands and feet in the fresh water, Midas remained in the main chamber. He lowered his massive body to the stone floor and bowed his head, pressing his brow against the cold rock, inhaling the scent of his greatest treasures: his family.

A dragon's hoard was meant to be a place of pride and a testament to his survival. But surrounded by gold and jewels and artifacts stolen from a world that hated him, Midas felt only hollow without them.

None of it mattered without them.

He exhaled a slow, shuddering breath, and something hot slid down the bridge of his snout and splashed against the stone.

Later, when the boys returned, Elowen ushered them

past him with gentle words and steady hands. Midas watched them go, resisting the instinct to reach out—to pull them close with his tail and promise them safety.

But promises meant nothing if the fear remained.

That night, Elowen joined him at the cave's mouth when the boys were asleep and the stars were high.

She sat beside his great head and rested her forehead against his scales. He turned his head slightly, careful not to jostle her, and rested his snout in her lap. She held him there as if he were small like the boys, and he leaned into her touch like it was the only thing keeping him alive.

She felt the grief in every breath he took, but held him anyway.

"Mama?" Kalen asked suddenly one morning, while the boys were helping Elowen brush her hair. "Why can't we go into the sky with Papa?"

Auric perked up at that, the same curiosity piquing him.

Elowen's heart twisted. She pressed a kiss to Kalen's hair, then another to Auric's brow, letting the warmth of them soothe the rising ache in her chest. She could lie, and their tender hearts would accept it, but it didn't feel right to hide this from them—not when the lie could cost them their lives.

She offered them the easiest answer first: "Well, I think your Papa still thinks your wings are too small for flight." She sighed, deciding to tell them the true reason as well.

"And because the world outside isn't kind to those who are different."

Auric frowned. "But we're just a family right? I thought that was good."

"It is," she whispered, stroking his back. "And you are perfect, as is our family. But not everyone sees the way your papa and I do. Some humans...they are afraid of what they don't understand."

"Are *you* afraid of us?" Kalen asked, voice small.

"Oh, never," she breathed. "I love you more than the moon loves the sky. But other humans haven't met you. All they would see is your strength. Your claws. Your wings. They would be afraid."

The boys sat in silence, their golden eyes wide.

"Your papa fears for you," she added gently. "He remembers what it felt like to be hunted. That day when the humans ambushed us at the lake, it broke your father. He blames himself for what happened. He would never forgive himself if anything happened to you again. He did not want you around the humans before, and he certainly doesn't want to risk it now."

"But *you're* human," Auric said, confused.

She nodded. "Yes, I am," she said softly. "But the other humans were not kind to me either. They hurt me because I tried to help your father when they tried to hurt him."

She lowered the collar of her dress to reveal her back down to her shoulder blades and turned to show them. She let them see the old scars mixed with the new ones, pale and pink across her skin.

Auric and Kalen gasped together, and Kalen asked: "They did that...because you helped Papa?"

"Yes," she said, throat tight. "Because I showed kindness. Because I tried to protect someone they feared. That was the last time I saw the humans that I grew up with. I did not see another human until they attacked us at the lake, and I haven't seen them since."

The boys sat very still for a moment. Then, quietly, they shifted closer. Kalen leaned forward first, nuzzling gently into her shoulder at the edge of one scar. Auric followed suit, purring against her back with a low, comforting chirr in his throat. They did it just like their father had done many times before.

Elowen's breath caught in her chest.

"You are so much of him," she whispered, smiling through the burn in her eyes. "But you're mine too. And I will never lie to you. You are both dragon and human, and one day, the world will learn to understand that." She turned back to them and gathered them in her arms. "But until then," she said, "you must stay close so we can protect each other."

They nodded solemnly, their foreheads pressed against hers.

Midas watched from the shadows beyond the hearth, watching as the boys comforted the woman who had once comforted him.

And later that night, while Midas was watching the stars near the mouth of the cave, he heard the small pitter-patter of young footsteps approaching.

He turned slowly, as though he was afraid he had imagined the sound. But his eyes immediately fell to Kalen, sheepishly standing next to him.

"Papa?" he said. Midas huffed for him to continue. "Are you cold?"

Midas blinked, but shook his great head slightly. There was a long pause before Kalen spoke again.

"Do you want to come back to the nest?"

Midas tensed slightly, for it was a gift far greater than his son understood. He answered with the rumble of the dragons:

Only if you want me there.

Kalen nodded, then reached out his small fingers to wrap around Midas' talon to tug, prompting him to follow, and Midas let himself be led.

When they reached the pile of blankets and pelts, Midas curled himself gently around the family once more. Elowen lay between the boys, and each of them reached toward him in sleep—one clutching his tail, the other curled near the crook of his arm.

Midas knew he would carry the scar of rejection for a long while after their young hearts moved on, but for tonight at least, the ache had finally lessened.

THIRTY-NINE

THE MORNING WAS COOL, the mountain air crisp with early mist. The forest stretched wide beneath the ridgeline, dotted with glimmers of light where the sun broke through the trees.

Kalen stood beside his father at the edge of a high overlook, his small hand gripping one of Midas' claws, both of them looking down at the world together.

Elowen had sent them out alone. Midas hadn't asked for it, and yet she somehow knew they needed it. Kalen's twin brother stayed behind with their mother, so there they were, father and son—dragon and hatchling.

Kalen stood beside his father, both in their smaller, humanoid forms, eyes sharp, instincts apt, observing the world like he knew the skies would belong to him one day.

He had still been apprehensive about his nature after what the humans did to him, but today, he had stopped being afraid. Today, he was curious.

Kalen nuzzled against his father, one horn scraping against Midas' scales, the other, a remaining stump barely protruding from his skull.

"You are warmer than mama," Kalen said absently.

Midas nodded. "That is because fire lives inside me."

"Can you always feel it?"

"Always. But it does not burn...it soothes. You will understand, little one, as you grow. Your fire is small now, like embers under the cooking fire, but one day, it shall burn hotter than all the fires in this world."

Kalen paused inquisitively. "Do you like it?"

"*Like* it?" Midas repeated. At first, he did not understand the question. Elowen *liked* to braid his hair. Midas *liked* to watch his children play. But he had never thought of the flame inside of him as anything other than...there. A truth. A part of him. Midas thought a bit longer before turning his golden eyes to his son. "I did not like it when I was alone. The fire inside me once meant anger, destruction, pain. It held memories that would have been a mercy to forget. But now...now my fire is protection. It is my legacy. It is my family. So no, my son, I do not like it, I respect it, for it has given me the most sacred thing I have ever known."

Kalen was quiet for a while. He settled further into his father's side, and Midas' tail wrapped around his son.

"Mama says there used to be other dragons, but they have been gone for a long time, and that's why you talk about being alone. She says you miss them a lot."

Midas didn't flinch, though the words hit him hard.

"It is true. Before you and your brother were born, I was the only dragon left. But I once had a mother, a father, and many brothers and sisters."

"Why did they leave you alone?"

Midas paused for an uncomfortable second. "They didn't leave. They were taken by the humans. What they did to you was only the beginning of what they did to the dragons. They think we are monsters."

"Do you hate humans?"

Midas turned away from the light of the sun, casting shadows of his horns across Kalen's face. "Yes."

"But mama is a human. And I am part human, right? Do you hate us too?" His eyes glossed over with unknown emotions overtaking his young heart.

Midas pulled Kalen closer to hold him. "I could never hate you, or your mother or Auric. It is true, your mother is human, and that makes you part human too. But your mother is proof of what the humans could be, if only they wanted to. She will raise you to be all the best of humanity, and I will raise you with all the might of the dragons." Kalen's lips continued to tremble, and so Midas leaned in to press his forehead to the crown of Kalen's head. "You are not lesser to me because you are part human, just as you are not a lesser dragon because the humans took one of your horns. You are not broken, you are mine."

Kalen finally curled into his father's embrace, and Midas wrapped his wings around them both. He sat there with his son for a while, staring at the stump where his horn had been cut from his body.

It was a stark reminder of one of his greatest failures—to see that they marked their son with cruelty in such a permanent way.

If only I had been stronger. If only I had been faster.

Midas huffed, smoke escaping from his human nostrils. Then, he leaned back so that he could speak to his son.

"Kalen, would you like to learn how to use your fire today?"

He perked up with disbelief. Midas had always told them they were still too young and fragile to learn, but he could not mask their instincts any longer, knowing it could protect them one day if the humans ever came for them again.

"Really?" Kalen asked.

Midas nodded. "Let us fetch your brother."

WITH THE DAYS warmer and the skies clearer, there were no better conditions to teach his sons about their true nature. Midas stood in his hulking dragon form in the ridge near the lake where he first met Elowen, and observed his boys for a while with new eyes.

With the village gone, there was no danger.

Auric and Kalen had grown leaner and taller in their human forms. They were still young boys, but were quickly shedding the last softness of early childhood. Their horns were longer and thicker. One pair unbroken, the other uneven and sharp but no less than the other. Whole, in its own way.

Midas nudged Elowen once, awaiting permission from the matriarch of their young pride. She nodded with a soft smile, and took a seat on the rock she had rested on so many times before. They both knew their boys were ready, and so Midas stepped into the clearing with his sons at his side.

Midas' dragon form was towering and regal, wings covering the glade like thunderclouds. By contrast, the boys were small and uncoordinated still in their dragon forms. They scarcely took the form, mostly for sleep or play, but never for learning.

But they looked up with awe in their eyes at their father, ready and eager for whatever he would teach them. Midas lowered his head and spoke in the dragon tongue, the deep tremble in his throat woven into words only the three of them could understand.

You have carried my fire from birth. The time has come for you to learn to use it.

The boys nodded. Midas turned to Auric first. *Try,* he commanded.

He gave no instruction, for he desired them to learn it from the instincts they were born with. The child closed his eyes, focusing. He inhaled for a long time, and on the exhale, a thin stream of flame spilled from his mouth—brief, hot, *perfect*. His eyes lit up.

Midas let out a low, proud growl. *Good. Your fire is elegant.*

Kalen stepped forward next, confidence in his stance. His fire came quicker. Wilder. It was a burst instead of a stream, and he stumbled back, blinking through the smoke, grinning despite himself.

Midas lowered his head. *Good. Your fire is fierce.*

Kalen's grin faltered slightly. *But it's so...angry.*

Midas met his eyes, serious and steady. *Rage is not evil. Rage is a response. When you channel it, it becomes protection. When you control it, it becomes strength.*

Elowen watched from the stone, her hands tangled in her hair as she braided flowers into the plait as she watched them.

Next came the lesson of flight. Midas stood behind them on the ridge and opened his wings wide. *Feel the air,* he said. *It is a part of you as the fire is. It wants to lift you. It wants you to protect the skies with me.*

The boys tried, extending their wings to their full span. Still small, but strong enough to carry them. At first, they stumbled. Wings flapped unevenly. Their bodies landed hard enough to leave divots in the dirt.

Midas did not laugh. He did not force them to try harder than they were willing. He simply encouraged them by helping them back to their feet when they stumbled.

Your wings are not just muscle and bone, he said. *Inside them is instinct. You were born for this.*

They tried again. And this time they rose. Not much. It was just a few feet. Just a few seconds. But both Kalen and Auric flew in small circles around their father's great head.

The sound that left Kalen's throat was half-laughter, half-roar. His brother's feet barely touched the ground as he spun midair, wings twitching.

Midas watched them from the ground, his heart full and silent. When they landed, breathless and panting, they ran to him. Not to Elowen. To *him.*

They wrapped their claws into the scales around his legs, laughing, shouting: *Did you see? Did you see?*

Midas crouched and gave them both an affectionate lick between their brows. *Yes my boys,* he said softly. *You were the most magnificent thing I've ever witnessed.*

They beamed, and Elowen, who had watched every moment, wept quietly into her hands with pride and love.

FORTY

Elowen sat in the shallow basin used for bathing, the hem of her underdress hitched up around her thighs. Her hair was unbound, floating slightly behind her as she leaned back, eyes closed, the tension slowly bleeding from her limbs.

She hadn't had a moment to herself like this in...she couldn't remember. Maybe never.

Elowen heard bare human footsteps behind her. She opened her eyes and turned just as Midas stepped into view —his humanoid form glowing faintly in the late light, his gold-kissed skin marked by faint traces of onyx scales. His tail trailed quietly behind him, relaxed.

He crouched beside the basin and tilted his head at her, smiling.

"Is Mama enjoying her moment of peace away from her little dragons?"

"I'm *bathing*," she corrected with a smirk.

His gaze dropped, sweeping over her exposed legs, the curve of her shoulder. "Then I've come to assist."

"The boys–"

"Are finishing their chores before I take them out flying again."

Elowen understood. This moment was for them, and there would be no interruptions. Midas reached forward, cupped his hands into the water, and poured it gently down her shoulder. She shivered beneath the warmth, watching the rivulets trail down her skin.

"You're good at learning," she whispered. "And teaching too, as we've discovered."

His hands trailed through the water again, then over her arms, gently. Her fingers found his jaw, traced the faint lines of his face.

"It's been a long time since it was just you and I."

His eyes softened. "I know."

She leaned into his hand. "We've been so focused on healing...on the boys..."

"And I would do it all again," he said. "Every second."

"I would too." She reached up and brushed a wet strand of hair from her face. "But I've missed you."

He kissed her then. The kind of kiss that didn't demand anything except to be *felt*.

"I'm right here, my heart," he whispered against her lips.

Her hands curled around his neck, pulling him closer, and he slid into the basin with her, shifting their bodies so she was resting in his lap as the water sloshed around their thighs. His forehead pressed to hers. His breath was slow and steady against her lips.

"I want more," she whispered.

He opened his eyes and cocked his head to the side in that curious way he did in his dragon form, following him in this state.

"I want to do it again. To build something new."

Midas stared at her. Not confused. Just stunned by the hope in her voice.

"You...wish for more children?" he asked, voice low.

"I do." She cupped his cheek. "I loved carrying them. Raising them. Watching them become themselves. And I see how you look at them, Midas. How proud you are. And it would be my honor to fill our pride with so many more of our perfect children."

His throat moved in a slow swallow. "I would love to have more," he said. "But you...are you sure, Elowen? The birth..."

He shuddered at the memory. Elowen leaned in, kissed him again—deeper this time. The wet fabric of her dress turned hot between them. She pressed her palm to his chest, right over his heart.

"I would go through it all again without a second thought, Midas."

They stayed like that in the water for a long time— trading kisses and touches, breath warming breath. Their moment winded down just as the twins came looking for them, and Midas left his mate with a loving kiss before taking to the skies with his sons once more.

THE CAVE WAS DIMLY LIT by the dying fire, its golden light flickering along the walls. The boys had long since fallen asleep, curled into each other like twin seeds tucked into the same earth. Their soft breaths rose and fell in perfect rhythm, wrapped in furs and dreams.

Midas lay behind Elowen on their shared nest of blankets, his arm draped loosely over her waist, his bare chest warm against her back. Elowen shifted slightly, pressing her hand to his where it rested against her stomach.

"Did you mean it?" she whispered.

His voice was low and quiet against the back of her neck. "Mean what?"

"When you said you wanted more children?"

He nodded against her skin. "There is no fire in the world strong enough to burn that wish from me."

Her breath hitched softly. She turned in his arms to face him, one leg sliding between his, her fingers ghosting over the ridge of his jaw. "I want to carry your children again, Midas. Even knowing what the world is."

His golden eyes met hers, wide and searching.

"I want it not in spite of the danger," she said, "but because of the love. Because we made something *beautiful*, even when the world tried to break it."

He ran his fingers along her stomach then. "The thought of you full with my child again..." His voice broke into a low hum.

She kissed him—soft and slow, her fingers tangling in his dark hair.

When they pulled apart, breathless, he rested his forehead to hers and whispered, he held her tighter. She rested her head beneath his chin, listening to his steady heart.

ONE MOON LATER

Elowen stirred from sleep, stretching beneath the blankets. She blinked, yawning softly, and turned to find Midas already awake beside her. He was in his human form, lying on his side, head propped against one hand. His golden eyes were fixed on her, and his tail was flicking around playfully with the same mischief in his eyes.

She smiled sleepily. "What?"

He reached out, brushed a loose strand of hair from her face, then slowly let his hand settle over her abdomen. Elowen's breath caught.

"I think you're carrying again," he said gently.

She blinked at him, confused, then laughed. "Midas, how would you know that?"

He didn't smile. "I smell it," he said. "Your scent has changed. Only slightly. But it's there, just like before. I feel it in you like I feel the fire in my throat."

She stared at him, wonder and disbelief flickering in her eyes.

"It's too early to tell," she said, but the words felt fragile now. Thin. "We've scarcely been trying for a cycle!"

He only looked at her with an unwavering and proud smile.

"Your body is building something new," he said. "I would know it anywhere."

She laid her hand gently over his, resting on her stomach. Her eyes softened. "We should tell the boys. They will be thrilled."

Later that morning, they sat outside near the lake. The boys were stacking stones, building some imagined fortress, arguing over whose side the turtle they'd found belonged to.

Elowen and Midas sat a few feet away on a flat rock warmed by sunlight. She looked over at him—he gave a small nod.

She turned to the boys. "Can we tell you two something?"

They both looked up, instantly alert. Kalen cocked his head. "Are we in trouble?"

Midas snorted softly. "Should you be?" he mused teasingly. The boys sank playfully into themselves.

Elowen laughed. "No. It's something...good." The boys exchanged a look, then trotted over and sat cross-legged in front of her, expectant. "I think we might be adding someone new to our family."

They blinked. Midas leaned forward, one arm around Elowen's back, the other resting loosely across his knee. "A sibling," he clarified.

Kalen's mouth dropped open. "You mean...a brother or sister?"

"Yes," Elowen said, smiling. "Your father suspects I might be pregnant."

"With another dragon baby?" Auric gasped.

Elowen laughed. "Yes."

There was silence for a moment. The boys looked at each other, then back at their parents. And then—*excitement.*

Kalen sat up straighter. "Can I teach them how to make fire?"

"I get to name them!" the other shouted.

"No way, I get first pick!"

The morning passed softly after that.

Elowen sat in the grass just beyond the cave, her dress gathered around her knees, a bundle of herbs in her lap waiting to be cleaned of dirt. The boys were nearby, lying flat on their bellies in the sun, drawing on the stone walls with charred rock.

They'd been quieter since the news, though not in a concerning way. It was more like they were trying to understand how their family would change with another member.

Kalen was the first to break the silence. "Where do babies come from?"

Elowen blinked, startled.

He turned to look at her, propping his chin in his hands. "Like...inside you? Like in the stories you tell? Is that real?"

His brother chimed in immediately. "Yeah. You said the baby might be in your belly, but how does it get there?"

Elowen smiled softly. She set the herbs aside and leaned back on her elbows, the sun warming her through the fabric of her dress.

"Well," she began, "babies do grow inside me. They start very, very small. A piece of me and a piece of your father come together to form something new. And that something grows, a little more each day, until it's ready to be born."

The boys stared at her like she was telling the beginning of a fairy tale.

"But how does it grow?" Kalen asked. "Does it eat what you eat?"

"Yes," she said. "It takes everything from me: food, water, sleep, warmth. It lives off what I give it. When I was pregnant with you both, I was always tired and my stomach never seemed to settle. But it's all worth it, and your father will watch over me to make sure I have everything I might need."

"Is it hard?" Auric asked, brows furrowing.

She nodded slowly. "Very hard. Carrying you two nearly broke my body. It hurt. A lot. But I would do it again a hundred times."

The boys went quiet again. Kalen rolled onto his side, eyes on her belly. "Will they grow their fire inside you?"

Elowen blinked. "What do you mean?"

He rubbed his palms together inquisitively. "I just think if the baby is a dragon like us, then...maybe it has fire inside it, too. And you get tired because it's learning to burn."

Elowen smiled. "I think you might be right."

"Is that why Papa got so mad when we were hurt?" Kalen's brother asked suddenly. "Because he saw what we did to you as babies?"

Elowen exhaled slowly. Her gaze turned toward the distant sky.

"Yes, but I wouldn't say it that way," she said, thinking his explanation sounded too harsh. "He watched me struggle to bring you into this world. He saw me bleed, and shake, and scream. And when they hurt you, he knew exactly how much it cost to grow you. He couldn't bear the thought of losing something that precious."

The wind stirred the grass. A hawk cried out far above. Kalen sat up slowly and shuffled across the thin blanket under her until he could curl beside her. His brother followed. They pressed their small bodies against her side, each resting a hand gently over her middle.

Soon after Elowen fell pregnant with her third child, growling filled the cave.

It was low and imperceptible; barely more than a rumble in the chest. It was the sound Midas used to make in his sleep when he dreamt of danger, memories stirring too loud in his bones.

But now, the sound came from the boys.

The first time it happened, Midas had approached Elowen while she was tending the fire—one hand resting absentmindedly on her lower belly, her face serene and drowsy with the quiet exhaustion of growing something new. He'd reached for her, quick and eager to greet her after returning from a long hunt.

And Kalen growled. He stepped between them, teeth bared, stance wide, like a wolf cub bristling before a shadow.

Midas stopped, startled. The boy blinked, confused by his own reaction—but didn't step aside. Elowen laid a hand gently on his shoulder. "It's all right, love. It's your father."

Kalen's body eased slightly, but his eyes stayed sharp.

It happened again two days later. This time, Midas came up behind Elowen while she was hanging herbs near the entrance of the cave. He placed a hand on her back—and both boys turned in unison, their small chests vibrating with the same low, instinctive warning.

It wasn't born of fear or defiance, but *protection*. They were *guarding* their mother.

Elowen chuckled, turning to glance at her mate. "You're going to have to stop sneaking up on me before they attack."

Midas didn't laugh at her teasing, and instead stared at his sons, feeling something inside of him bloom.

And by the week's end, they were bringing her food.

It was usually small things—handfuls of berries, roots clumsily cleaned, dried mushrooms piled beside her blanket. They hovered when she ate, watching intently, nudging more toward her if she so much as paused.

Elowen shot Midas an amused glance as he returned from cleaning fish at the cave's entrance, her boys close behind, carrying the baskets for her.

"They've declared themselves the official attendants of my womb," she whispered.

Midas didn't answer at first. He only crouched beside them, watching as one of the boys carefully pressed a warm stone against her feet to ease her soreness.

Nothing could match the beauty of this: his sons, dragon-blooded and born in a world so cruel, choosing tenderness not because they were told to, but because they had seen Midas love Elowen this way, and so they treated the mother of their pride with the same care and respect.

Because they knew, in their bones, that she was everything to them. Midas reached out and rested a clawed hand on Kalen's head. The boy looked up, eyes shining.

"You are becoming men," Midas said softly. "You are learning what it means to protect something not out of fear, but because it is precious."

Both boys nodded solemnly.

"She's our mother," the younger one said. "She made us. She makes more of us."

"She has fire too," Kalen added. "Just...a different kind."

Midas looked at Elowen. Her eyes were wet.

LAUGHTER ECHOED THROUGH THE CAVERN, bright and wild and wholly alive.

It started as a flick of a tail, a playful swipe of a claw. One of the twins, Kalen, had darted beneath Midas' great foreleg, squealing with delight as Auric launched from a rock ledge and landed squarely on his father's back with a tiny roar.

Midas twisted his serpentine neck with exaggerated slowness, golden eyes wide in mock offense. He let out a growl, low and rumbly, the kind that once sent whole villages scattering.

The boys only giggled in their dragon forms, having learned to easily shift without the exasperation that plagued their father when he did the same.

You dare challenge me? he said in the old tongue with feigned offense.

They shrieked and fled as he gave chase, wings half-unfurled and scraping the cavern roof, talons tapping against stone as he lunged and rolled with a grace only a creature of his age and size could wield.

Auric was caught first, scooped up in a massive claw and deposited—gently, *always* gently—into the unrelenting curl of Midas' tail.

Kalen tried to climb his father's tail to save his brother, only to yelp when it lifted and flipped him neatly onto his back with a *thump* of giggling limbs.

They squirmed and rolled and roared their tiny roars, pouncing and biting in mock battle. Their dragon instincts blossomed so easily—those flashes of strength and wildness that pulsed just beneath their baby skin.

Midas gave them the space to stretch into it, and it healed something deep inside him. For the first time in a century, he felt like *himself*.

His boys didn't flinch from his size. They weren't afraid of his fire. They climbed his scales and tangled in his tail and shouted challenges in half-spoken words.

Elowen stood by the hearth, her eyes glowing with fond exasperation as she folded a blanket and called out warnings that went gleefully ignored.

Kalen's tail knocked over a pile of furs with a triumphant squeal. Auric scrambled after him on all fours, claws clattering on stone as he pounced. The two boys were nothing if not chaos incarnate—gold-eyed, fire-blooded, and boundless in energy. They were strong. Growing fast, but not yet careful of their inhuman size and instincts.

Elowen knelt beside the fire pit, stirring a small pot of stew. Her hair was loose, her sleeves rolled, and though her back was turned, her laughter, light and unguarded, drifted toward her boys like smoke.

Then, too quick to stop, Kalen leapt.

He tackled her from behind with a wild shriek, not yet understanding the weight of his own body. Auric followed suit, giggling, his scaled feet skidding across the stone as he flung his wings around her waist.

They knocked her flat to the floor. A sharp gasp escaped her, the pot clattering nearby. For a breathless second, all was still.

Then Midas was moving.

Enough, he growled, the word firm as thunder.

The boys froze. Midas was across the cave in a heartbeat, kneeling beside Elowen as she caught her breath. She waved him off, coughing once but smiling.

"I'm fine," she said, brushing hair from her face. "Just got the wind knocked out of me."

But her laugh, soft as it was, couldn't hide the tremor in her limbs or the startled flutter of her heartbeat. Her hand felt her middle, and Midas gave her a gentle nudge that told her she had nothing to fear— that they did not do any lasting harm to her or the baby.

Midas turned to the boys. Their shoulders drooped. Kalen looked guiltily at his claws; Auric wouldn't meet his eyes.

You are not like her, Midas said in the old tongue, the weight of his words sinking deep into the stone. *She is soft. Small. You must not treat her as you treat me, especially while she carries a child in her belly. Do you understand?*

Kalen blinked. *But we were playing.*

I know, my son, but you mustn't play with her with the same energy as you play with me.

They looked down, ashamed, but knowing they were not truly in trouble.

Elowen, ever merciful, reached out and pulled them both into a gentle hug. "It's alright," she said with a tired smile. "I can handle a cave full of roughhousing boys. Just... maybe not all at once, alright?"

"I'm sorry, mama. We didn't mean to hurt you," Auric mumbled, having shifted back to apologize, his voice so small it made Midas' chest ache.

"I know, sweetling," she murmured, kissing the top of his head. "And I love you both, wild claws and all."

Both boys snuggled close to her, curling up in her lap like oversized kittens. Midas lowered himself beside her. He stroked her arm once with his snout, just to feel that she was warm and unharmed.

"I *can* handle it," she whispered again, quieter this time, meant only for him. "But thank you for reminding them. For protecting me."

His golden eyes met hers, and he nodded. She smiled, leaning into his side.

Later, when the fire had dimmed and the game had worn the boys into soft little puddles of scales and dreams, Midas curled himself into a slow, protective coil.

The twins clambered up his nose like a mountain trail, finding their sleeping place at last between the great ridges of his brow and the base of his horns. One snuggled into the warm space beneath his golden crest, the other curled into the dip above his eyes like a living crown.

Elowen tucked herself against his chest. He wrapped his tail around her without a word. She sighed into the warmth of his scales, brushing a kiss to the underside of his jaw before settling in, her head resting against the rhythmic thrum of his heart.

The boys snored softly. Elowen's breath slowly evened out. And Midas stayed perfectly still, afraid that if he moved —if he even breathed too loudly—that this impossible, undeserved happiness might all vanish.

His eyes closed, and his heart, ancient and battle-scarred, whispered thanks to whatever gods still listened.

FORTY-TWO

The stench of humans was particularly vile. Acrid. Smoke, sweat, and iron.

The village to the north of Elowen's old home had outgrown their walls, and they had begun to encroach on the mountain.

Midas stalked through the cover of fog, wings pressed tight against his sides as his talons carved deep grooves into the soft, wet dirt. He kept low, his golden eyes glinting under the moonlight as he prowled at the edge of the forest. The wind was favorable tonight, blowing more fog across him to obscure his frame.

He comes to watch them every night, to ensure they did not get too close to his cave, his nest, his *family*.

He exhaled thick smoke through his nostrils, the embers of his breath scattering through the dense fog. The sound of his heart was steady, until there was a small rustle behind him. Too heavy for an animal, too quick for a human.

His head snapped around, his pupils narrowing into slits. He breathed in deep the air around him, and the smell finally reached him.

Familiar. Warm. *Infuriating.*

A snarl ripped from his throat, and two small shapes froze in the tree line. Barely shadows against the woods, but Midas could see the scales glinting faintly under the moonlight, just enough to betray them through the fog.

He lunged. Both boys yelped and tried to run, but Midas was faster. His talons caged their bodies to the ground, careful not to harm, but harsh enough that they could not twist free. Their frightened little sounds pierced something deep in him, but the fury burning in his chest drowned it out.

He didn't roar at them—he *erupted.* The ancient language of the dragons resonated through his throat from deep in his chest.

What are you doing here? he demanded. His voice was thunder, echoing through the trees and scaring away the birds. *You followed me? Here? To this cursed place?*

Neither boy answered. Instead, they trembled, but Midas did not notice.

Do you have any idea what the humans would do if they saw you? Have you already forgotten what they did to us the last time they found us together? His growl shook the earth beneath them again. *And what of your mother, hm? You would leave her alone in such a delicate state?*

No answers came from the boys, only terrified whimpers. Midas could not hear them over his own rage. He let them free, only to take their tails between his teeth, lifting them from the ground and carrying them toward the mountain. The boys cried out, their voices sharp with fear as their father carried them like prey.

Elowen was waiting when he landed at the mouth of their cave, relief flooding her features to see her children again. They likely snuck away and worried her sick.

"Midas?" she breathed, rushing toward the three of them.

Midas dropped the boys onto the cave floor, with enough force that they stumbled. They scrambled away immediately, hiding behind their mother's legs. Their little chests heaved, and their eyes were wide with terror, barely peeking out from under her skirt.

A piece of fabric was no shield though, and Midas continued his barrage of rage on the boys, screaming at them in a language Elowen could not understand or replicate with her human throat.

His voice boomed through the cave walls, making the stones quake. *I told you never to leave the ridge without me! How dare you disobey me!*

Elowen squatted to wrap her arms around her boys, pulling them tight against her. "Midas, stop."

Midas lifted his head and sent a growl in her direction, a warning, before turning his attention back to his children. *You endangered your mother. You endangered all of us! What do you have to say for yourselves?*

"Midas, they are children," Elowen snapped, her own voice suddenly sharp enough to slice through his rage. "They are your *children*. Look at them!"

He does look, for a moment, at his sons. At the small, trembling bodies pressed against their human mother's legs. At the tears brimming in their bright golden eyes. They had shifted back into their human forms, and looked up at their father with...*fear.*

They were *afraid* of him.

Midas exhaled, smoke dissipating into the air. His claws dug into the stone under him. His wings, still tense with anger, slowly lowered until they drooped heavily with shame.

Elowen, still shielding the boys with her body, lowered her voice. "You're scaring them," she said softly, her tone gentle but firm. "They don't understand why you're shouting. Right now, they only see their father acting with fire and fury. They are small, Midas."

Midas turned his head away, for he could not meet her eyes any longer. His chest felt tight, as if his ribs were the only thing keeping the guilt from gnawing straight through his hide.

I was only trying to keep them safe, he said, but he knew Elowen could not understand the language of the dragons. When he opened his eyes, he looked to Kalen and Auric, hoping they heard him.

They were still staring, eyes still wide with fear.

A low rumble vibrated in Midas' throat. Exhaustion from his own fear began dwindling, so he could finally see what he had done. He lowered himself until he was eye-level with his sons, his great head dipping toward the ground in submission.

I am sorry, he said softly to them, his words heavy in his chest. The boys did not answer, nor did he expect them to. They simply stayed behind the safety of their mother, hiding from him.

He lowered his head further, resting it completely

against the stone ground. For the first time in a long while, Midas felt powerless. Not against the humans, but against the simple, fragile love of his family.

He realized in that moment that he was not roaring in anger as he thought, it was because he was terrified of losing them.

But they did not know that, and so Midas had done the opposite of what he intended, and terrified *them* instead.

THE CAVE WAS QUIET NOW, only the faint drip of water from the ceiling, and the soft rhythm of his children breathing in their nest.

Midas laid near the entrance of their cave, his wings folded tight against his sides. His head was bowed low as he stared into the dark with his golden eyes. He had not moved for hours, not even to warm the bedtime nest with the great fire in his heart.

Elowen joined him only after she was sure the boys were fast asleep. The echo of her bare feet on the stone was louder than it should be in the uncomfortable silence of their home.

"Midas," she said softly. "You should come and rest."

He huffed in response. She knelt next to him, sighing in relief at his familiar warmth. His large eyes flickered to his mate, so small in comparison to him, yet never afraid to approach.

"You frightened them," she said, as if he didn't already know it.

Midas, after a long moment, shifted into his human form so he could speak to her. She waited for him to join her, sitting quietly at the edge of the cave.

"They disobeyed me." His voice rumbled low in his chest. "They followed me to the humans. Don't you understand what that could have meant? What could have happened if they were seen?"

"I do," Elowen said. "But screaming at them until they cower behind me is not the same as protecting them."

His nostrils flared, the terror of what could have happened still haunting him. "They needed to understand–"

"Understand that their father is something to be afraid of?"

Midas' head snapped up, the gold of his eyes sharpening. "They should be afraid! Fear keeps you alive. Fear tells you when to run, when to hide, when to stay quiet. Fear is what saved me when–" He stopped suddenly, quieting his voice. "When I was a hatchling and the humans attacked, my mother, my siblings, they did not have enough fear, and they were slain. I *survived* because I was *afraid*."

Elowen's expression softened, but she didn't look away. He looked away instead, his gaze sinking to the floor. His claws scraped at the stone like he was trying to carve his guilt into it.

"I *cannot* lose them," he murmured. "Not them. Not you. Not us."

"You won't," Elowen said, moving closer. Her fingers

hovered over his chest, then rested lightly against the warmth there. "But you can't let your fear speak louder than your love."

He closed his eyes at her touch, his breath shuddering through his chest. "I do not know the difference."

"I know," she whispered. "That's why I'm telling you now." She brushed her thumb over the edge of one of his scales on his chest, and his body trembled. "When they followed you, they weren't trying to defy you. They wanted to be like you. To be brave. To see what their father sees. To share the skies with you as you've always wanted. And you shouted at them for that."

Midas opened his eyes again, the gold in them dimmer now, wounded. "They could have died."

Elowen did not answer, because she knew he had to understand in his own way. It was not something she could explain with words. He let out a low sound—half growl, half broken exhale—and pressed his head to hers.

"I do not know how to be soft," he admitted, his voice cracking like firewood. "I never wished to make them afraid of me."

"I know."

The silence that followed was deep, but it was different this time. No longer cold or empty, but heavy with mutual understanding. Elowen kept her hand on his chest until his breathing slowed.

She stayed with him until the night faded toward morning, her body pressed against the warmth of his, his tail curling faintly around her like an unspoken apology.

Midas did not sleep, not after Elowen's voice faded to

silence and her hands fell still against his scales, and not after he carried her to bed and placed her in the nest next to Auric and Kalen.

Midas watched the glow of the fire dim and listened to the breaths of his sons rise and fall in soft unison. Every exhale wounded him. Every inhale tightened the guilt in his chest.

He had roared at them. Roared with fear disguised as fury.

He'd seen the terror in their eyes, and they had not looked at him as father or protector. They had looked at him as prey looked upon fire. He hadn't meant to scare them, and yet he had.

It was morning when he finally lifted his head to the sound of rustling. Elowen was still asleep, but the boys were awake. Their golden eyes were wide and uncertain, flicking from his claws to his teeth that he had used on them in rage.

They were still afraid. Midas' stomach twisted.

He lowered himself intentionally, making himself as small as he could in his weaker, human form, trying to be less threatening. His mouth opened to speak, and the boys immediately tensed.

"I am sorry," he started. "You disobeyed me, but I was... too loud, too harsh, but not because I was angry. I did not mean to frighten you, I was just...*afraid.*"

Kalen furrowed his brow. "Of us?"

Midas shook his head. "No. I was once small and curious like you, and the humans took everything from me. I was afraid of losing you, too."

They blink together. "You yelled at us," Auric said, his words shaking.

Midas paused. He did not know what to say. He simply huffed out: "Yes."

"The humans have never yelled at us," Kalen added, and it was a well-deserved sting.

Midas bowed his head lower. "I know. And I am...sorry."

The boys exchanged a glance, and then, slowly, Kalen crept closer. Just a step. Just enough to reach out and touch the edge of Midas' wing. Auric followed his brother, sitting cross-legged by Midas' other wing. "Can you tell us what it was like when you were little?"

Midas paused, furrowing his brow. "You want...a story?"

"Yeah," they said together.

The request is so ordinary, so innocent, like they had immediately forgotten why they were afraid. Midas glanced once toward Elowen, still sleeping, and then curled his tail gently around his sons.

"Do you remember what it was like before?" Kalen prompted as he felt the scales lining his father's human arm.

Auric shifted slightly, balancing himself on Midas' tail. "Before the humans," he added curiously.

Their words struck deeper than they should, not because they were sharp, but because they were curious and innocent.

How could they understand? They were born from all the love and warmth the world could offer them—born beneath a sky unmarked by their fear. Midas would not dare to give them a story that would give them that fear, but they were still young and curious as all boys were.

He could not hide the truth from them forever.

Midas closed his eyes. For a long time, he did not speak, and instead imagined the world long before they drew their first breaths. A low rumble rose from deep in his chest, thick with smoke and sorrow.

"I remember fire," he began. Kalen and Auric both fell silent and alert at his words. "It was not brutal, raging fire. It danced along the mountainside. It warmed our nests. The dragons lived in these very mountains. *So many* dragons that we could block out the sun itself with our bodies. Before the humans thought our roars were the sounds of monsters, they thought it was song. Song that could shake ice from the mountaintops. Song that called storms. Song that summoned the stars and the moon."

He did not have the heart to tell them how the humans began to hate their songs, nor did he describe the way they killed the young and mothers first. How they laid traps and laughed as the songs turned to terrified roars.

He did not have the heart to speak of the blood he could somehow still smell—a scent that never left his scales.

Yet somehow, Midas knew his boys understood that much without him having to say it. It was in their bones— the trauma of their father seeped into their lives from conception. He could feel it in their silence, all the things they wanted to ask, but didn't know how.

"And you were alone," Kalen added, remembering how Midas told him as much.

Midas nodded. "Yes."

"For how long?" Auric asked.

"Too long," Midas answered quickly, but then looked

down at his children and softened his face. "Until I met your mother."

Their developing minds did not possess the strength to fathom how many years that was. But Auric's face lit up at the mention of Elowen, for he was always closer to her in his constitution. Softer, quieter, gentler.

Midas lowered his head to nuzzle each boy individually, wrapping his tail more tightly around them both.

"She may not have dragon blood in her veins, but she is still dragon. She is...the very foundation of this family. From her heart and body came a new era of dragons. *You*. Us. I would endure it all again if I knew she was waiting for me at the end."

THE SCENT of warm stone and damp moss drifted over Elowen before the first flicker of light broke through her sleep. She stirred slowly, blinking past the haze of dreams into the golden hue of morning. The fire had long since died down, leaving only the faintest ember glow pulsing like a heartbeat in the ash.

But it wasn't the fire that woke her. It was the sound. Low. Rumbling. Almost like thunder, but gentler.

She lifted her head from the nest and found herself staring into a vision she might once have believed belonged only in the stories of old if not for the way her heart lifted at the sight.

Midas lay curled along the stone floor in a crescent,

wings tucked in tight, tail coiled protectively around the two small figures nestled between his limbs.

Auric was perched like a king between his father's horns, legs dangling lazily on either side of the great crown of bone. Kalen lounged along the bridge of Midas' massive snout, his chin propped on his folded arms, dark hair ruffled and eyes alight.

Midas was speaking, and they were listening.

Whatever he said, it was not in words Elowen knew. Not in any human tongue. But in the rich, resonant language of dragons—deep and musical, like mountains shifting beneath the sea. The sounds rolled through the cave like velvet thunder, low and lulling, and the boys responded with small delighted noises, coos and soft giggles that melted against the stone. Elowen didn't understand a single word. But it didn't matter.

She watched from the shadows, heart full to bursting, as Midas wove some ancient tale only his kind could tell. He spoke slowly, his tone wrapping around each word like a secret. And her sons listened like they were being handed the stars.

With a quiet exhale, she pushed herself upright and padded softly to the edge of the hearth. She didn't wish to interrupt. She simply began preparing breakfast with quiet hands, grinding dried grains and crushed root into a thick porridge in the small stone bowl they kept tucked away.

The occasional giggle from Kalen broke through the steady rhythm of her stirring. Auric leaned forward, whispering something to his brother, and Midas snorted softly in amusement, the puff of smoke escaping his nostrils rising in a playful spiral.

Elowen wiped the corners of her eyes with the back of her wrist before the tears could fall into the food.

It was in these tender moments that filled her heart with so much joy, to see a family she never thought she would have living as though the cruelty of the world didn't exist.

And so she let them have it a little longer.

FORTY-THREE

Elowen awoke curled in Midas' arms, the familiar warmth of him pressed to her back. But her body was wrong—tight with discomfort, her stomach cramping in slow, sickening waves. She gasped, barely audible, but Midas stirred instantly.

"Elowen," he whispered, sitting up.

She clutched at her abdomen. "Something's wrong."

The scent hit him then. Blood.

Midas didn't ask questions. He gathered her into his arms, laid her carefully on a pile of furs separate from the boys, and lit the fire brighter with a sharp breath of heat.

She bled for hours, quietly wincing so she didn't disturb her sons despite her heart screaming in agony. She knew what was happening—they both did. But to speak it into existence made it real, and neither of them were ready to face it yet.

Midas held her hand when her body shook with pain. He whispered to her when the worst of it passed, his forehead pressed to hers, his voice a soft stream of love and apology. She cried without sound. He cleaned the blood from her carefully.

The next morning, the boys bounded toward them at the mouth of the cave, laughing, arms full of wildflowers and bits of bark they'd carved into toy animals.

"Look what we made for the baby!" Kalen shouted.

Elowen sat by the fire, wrapped in a thick blanket. Her face was pale. Midas stood nearby, unmoving. The boys approached eagerly. She covered her mouth with one hand. The other trembled in her lap. The boys stopped.

Auric looked up at Midas. "Papa?"

Midas knelt, slowly, lowering himself to their eye level. His expression was soft, but hollowed.

"I need you to listen," he said. They quieted instantly. "There is no easy way to say this." He paused, glanced at Elowen, then back to them. "The life your mother carried... it is gone."

The silence that followed stabbed her in the chest.

Auric blinked. "Gone?"

Elowen lowered her hand to her womb, still cramping and already feeling empty. Her voice was barely there. "I lost the baby."

Kalen stared at her. "No," he said sharply. "You're wrong. We made food. We made toys."

Midas touched his shoulder as Auric stepped forward, tears already in his eyes. "Where did they go?"

Elowen's throat closed. "I don't know, sweetheart."

Kalen dropped the toy in his hand. It hit the stone floor with a dull clatter. And then he ran off, deeper into the cave.

Later, long after the sun had fallen behind the ridge,

Elowen sat outside the cave alone. She clutched the small wooden carving Kalen had dropped, her thumb running along its uneven edges.

Midas found her there.

"I can't stop thinking," she whispered, "about how much they loved someone who never had a name."

Midas nodded.

"Do you think they'll hate me for this?"

"No," he said. "They are hurting. But they could never hate you."

She closed her eyes. "I don't know how to help them understand."

"You don't need to. They are young, their hearts are fiery like mine," he said softly. "They will come back to you when they are ready to learn more."

THE TOYS REMAINED UNTOUCHED. The fire burned low. The laughter that once rang through the stone corridors had faded into silence.

Elowen sat on the fur-lined nest, her knees drawn up to her chest, arms wrapped around them. She had braided her hair to keep her hands busy, but her fingers trembled. Her eyes were dry, but only because even tears had abandoned her.

The boys stood a few feet away, fidgeting. Nervous. Eyes flickering between her and each other. Finally, Kalen spoke:

"Why did it die?"

Elowen looked up slowly and swallowed. "Sometimes... things like this happen. Even when everything seems right."

"But it was safe," Kalen said. "You were eating. Sleeping. We brought you food. We helped."

"I know," she said softly.

"Then..." He hesitated. "Was it...something you did?"

She stilled. She knew in her heart things like this happened, but it was no easier to bear that guilt, because she asked herself that question every second that passed.

"Maybe you moved too much," his brother whispered. "Or got too tired. Or what if...what if when we knocked you down we hurt it?"

Elowen's throat closed. Her heart lurched. "No," she said, firmer now. "No, my loves. I didn't do anything to make this happen. None of us did."

"Then why?" Kalen cried. "Why would it leave if we were ready? If we loved it?"

The words shattered her. She reached for them, but neither stepped forward. They were confused. Hurting. Wanting to blame something, *anything*, the way young hearts do when they can't make sense of pain.

She took a slow breath. "My loves," she said, her voice shaking, "you did everything right. I did everything I could. But sometimes...life is fragile even when it's surrounded by love."

They looked at her, wide-eyed and uncertain.

"And it hurts," she continued. "Because we wanted them. So badly. But their body couldn't stay. Not because of anything we did. Not because we weren't good enough."

Kalen's brow furrowed. "Then what was the point?"

Tears finally welled in her eyes. She smiled through them, aching. "The point," she said, "is that they were real. Even if they were only with us for a short time, they were loved. They were part of our family, and we will always remember them."

Auric moved forward. He didn't cry. He just pressed himself into her lap, resting his head against her chest, like he used to when he was smaller.

"I didn't mean to make you sad."

She held him, breathing in the scent of his hair. "You didn't," she murmured. "You're allowed to ask questions."

His brother came next, crawling into her other side. Together, they curled against her like they did so often. And she, who had grown and carried them, held the living warmth of her children and let herself mourn the one she'd lost.

MIDAS WAS GUARDING the cliff just outside the cave when his sons approached. The sun had started to dip, casting the trees in coppery shadow. Smoke rose in curling wisps from his nostrils, and the scent of ash drifting in the breeze.

The boys came quietly—unusual for them. Just two pairs of small, determined feet padding softly over the stone. They stood side by side, staring at him with matching expressions: hopeful and uncertain.

They both shifted into their dragon forms and found comfortable positions curled in their father's warmth.

Papa?

Midas opened his eyes once more and huffed out a sound for them to continue.

Auric looked up. *Can you give Mama another baby? It will make her feel better.*

The question hung in the air like smoke. Midas didn't answer right away. He looked between them—so eager to help. Their faces held no malice. They simply didn't yet understand that love, no matter how pure, could not undo grief.

I know you were excited, he said gently. *I was too.* They nodded. *But making a baby isn't like carving a toy or planting a flower. It's more complicated than that.*

Kalen frowned. *But you and Mom already did it. Twice.*

Yes, Midas said with a soft smile. *And you are the greatest joy of both our lives. But your mother...she carries those children. In her body. In her blood. And sometimes, when things go wrong, it hurts her in ways we can't always see.*

They looked at each other, quiet.

She didn't do anything wrong, Midas continued. *But her heart and body need time to heal and rest.* Midas' chest ached. *I would give your mother a thousand children if it were her wish, but it must be hers. It must be something she asks for—not something we ask of her.*

The boys looked down at their claws. Kalen's voice was smaller now. *I don't want her to be sad.*

I know, but that is not the way to make her happy again. She doesn't need a baby to feel joy again. She has you. Your laughter. Your questions. So I want you to live and grow strong. Remind her that she is already surrounded by love.

Midas leaned forward and touched his forehead to each

of theirs, one at a time. A dragon's blessing. Ancient and sacred.

That is how we help heal her.

THAT NIGHT, when the cave had gone quiet and the boys were curled beneath blankets near the fire, Midas stirred in the dark.

He turned his great head to find Elowen sitting upright beside him, her hand pressed flat to her lower belly, her face turned away.

Tears streamed down her cheeks in silence.

He perked up slowly with attention. She shook her head, unable to meet his eyes.

"It just...hit me again," she whispered.

He leaned into her, and she leaned back into him like a wave folding into the shore, her body shuddering. She pressed her face to his neck, sobbing softly into the space between his neck and shoulder.

You are not broken, he murmured. *You were the home that baby knew. And even if they didn't stay, they were loved every moment they existed. You are still the mother of this new age of dragons and miracles.*

Her breath hitched, and though she couldn't understand his language, she felt every word in her bones as if he had spoken them directly into her ear.

And then slowly, *slowly,* she began to still with sleep.

FORTY-FOUR

THE BLOOD SMELL lingered on Elowen long after it stopped leaving her body.

It clung to the stone, to the air, to his scales—thin and metallic, sharp enough to sting the back of his throat. Midas did not know how long he had been curled around Elowen after it happened. Minutes, hours, days—time lost meaning when grief hollowed him out.

He could only remain where he was, wings curved protectively around her trembling body, afraid that if he loosened his hold even slightly, she might vanish like smoke.

She lay curled upon herself, small and silent, the steady rise and fall of her breath the only sign of life. Her scent had changed—no longer threaded with the faint, bright spark of new possibility he had sensed before, but muted with sorrow. It was a scent that stirred old memories in him, memories of dragon mothers whining softly over unhatched eggs.

Slowly, he became aware of something wrong inside himself, too.

The flame at the core of his chest, usually alive and coiled like a serpent of heat, flickered weakly. It felt distant, as though buried under layers of stone. When he attempted a breath of fire, only a thin curl of smoke escaped, wavering like a dying ember. Panic twitched along his ribs; instinct whispered danger. His fire was his warmth, his life, his strength. Dragons did not weaken unless wounded—or grieving.

He had not been struck. Not poisoned. Not hunted. But something inside him had fractured when he felt Elowen's pain tear through her.

He folded a wing more tightly over her, instinctively shielding her from cold, from danger, from the world. His body trembled with the effort and the unfamiliar weight of despair. He had survived centuries alone, but he had never known this helplessness that gnawed at him from within.

Elowen shifted weakly, pressing closer without waking. He felt the soft brush of her fingers against his scales, seeking warmth and comfort. He curved his body around her in answer, though the motion sent a shiver down his spine. His strength was draining like water through cupped claws.

Midas had a suspicion that his condition was due to his constant shifting. His human form was unnatural and awkward for him, even after all this time. Though his sons were born with the innate ability to shift, his changes were marked by indescribable pain and lingering weakness.

But Midas would endure that pain if it meant he could comfort Elowen with words and gestures that were more familiar to her in his human form. To move away from her now to rest and replenish his strength felt impossible.

And so he remained perfectly still, wings curved like a sheltering cave around the only creature left in the world who mattered.

He listened to her breath along with his own. Hers was soft and uneven. His grew quieter each hour. He bowed his head over her and let his eyes sweep across her and their children.

All night.

Even as the fire inside him continued to dim.

FORTY-FIVE

MIDAS NOTICED the changes in his body before anyone else did.

A dropped bowl that didn't quite get caught in time. A wince when bending to lift one of the boys. A flicker of irritation in his eyes when someone asked for something when he was trying to relax.

Midas had been shifting into his human form every sunrise for weeks now—longer than ever before. His horns and tail remained, a tether to his truer self, but the rest of him was soft and tired and wrong. His blood felt slow. His breath shallow. His strength was leaving him, quietly, like steam escaping through cracks.

But Midas was a stubborn creature, and so he did not give himself the time to heal his exhausted body. Elowen still cried in the night. His boys still wanted to roughhouse with him. He still needed to hunt for meat and patrol the skies to ensure his den was safe. These were things only he could do, and so he forced himself to be strong for his family.

But that strength required the fire inside him that only guttered lower each day with every shift.

One morning, he was near the cave's entrance after returning from a hunt. The limp deer fell from his teeth and he couldn't stop himself from collapsing to the cave floor. He told himself he would rest for only a moment.

Just a moment...

The boys were the ones that found him, bounding toward him with their endless energy, ready to beg to take to the skies with him.

Their intuition told them there was something wrong with Midas before they approached. They had never seen him slumped over in this state. Whenever Midas slept, he was always somehow still alert—but this was different. He did not move when the boys climbed over his body, and did not answer them when they nudged him.

Kalen made his way to the top of his head, between his horns, and snuggled into the space where it had always been warm before. This time though, Kalen felt the absence of heat, and his instincts instantly put him on alert.

Auric, he said. *Papa is cold.*

At first, Auric thought Kalen was teasing and that Midas was simply asleep, but then he looked closer. His chest rose and fell in shallow, shaky breaths, and when Auric moved closer, he too felt that unnatural coldness radiating from Midas' body where he had only felt warmth before.

Auric nuzzled Midas' face with his own. *Papa?*

When Midas didn't respond, Auric ran straight to his mother, heart stuttering and his mind racing with fear of the unknown. As he came up to his mother, washing a bowl in a basin of water, he shifted and frantically tugged on Elowen's skirt.

"Mama, Papa is cold."

Elowen hummed, not understanding. "What do you mean?"

Auric tugged her again, more aggressively this time, enough to make her stumble. "Come look!"

She followed her son to the mouth of the cave, where panic immediately overtook her at the sight of Midas. She dropped to her knees beside him, hands cupping his face.

"Love," she whispered. "Midas. Look at me."

He tried. He did. But he was fading.

"What happened? Are you hurt?"

He shook his head, barely.

I wanted... His voice cracked. *To stay close. To hold you.*

She looked to her boys for translation, and then tears began to well in her eyes. "You have held me," she said, tears spilling over. "But you're burning out. You need rest."

The boys clung to each other behind her, terrified, silent.

Elowen pressed her forehead to his. "Please."

He tried to stand, but instead slumped, exhausted, his great head resting on the ground beside her. The boys rushed forward, pressing themselves to his massive chest, feeling the unnaturally slow thump of his heart.

Elowen stood, stroking the side of his face.

He closed his eyes, drifting into rest forced upon him by exhaustion.

MIDAS SLEPT for nearly two days—scales pulsing faintly with heat, wings curled tight around his body, heart beating slow and heavy beneath his ribs.

Elowen never left his side.

She cleaned the cold sweat from his brow. She stroked his neck after. She wrapped his tail in blankets to protect it from the chill, and whispered to him in the dark when his breathing stuttered.

And the boys became guardians in their own right.

They took turns bringing him water and meat like they'd watched Elowen do. They lied against his side when he trembled in his sleep. They collected smooth stones and carved little sigils into them that Midas had taught them—symbols of protection, healing, flame, and family.

"He always watches us," Kalen whispered. "Now we watch him."

Elowen wept quietly at those words, brushing their hair back with shaking hands. And yet, something cold was stirring in her gut. If any of the humans had seen him in this state, or even suspected that he could be weak, they would come for their nest. And the boys, still too young, would not be able to fight off the humans themselves if they came.

This worry weighed heavily on Elowen, who knew first-hand of the cruelty of the humans, and every time the cave shifted, she flinched.

AFTER TWO MORE DAYS, the wind changed.

Elowen noticed how still the air had become. How the birds had stopped calling. How even the bees avoided the growing flowers at the cave mouth. Midas stirred that night, groggy and weak.

He rasped what she had assumed was her name in the language of the dragons. She leaned in. "I'm here."

Against his better judgement, and against Elowen's frantic protests, Midas shifted into his human form once more. She held his head against her chest, and when he looked up at her, his even his eyes seemed duller.

"You don't need to exhaust yourself," Elowen begged. "The boys and I managed while you were resting. We are okay."

"How long?"

She ran her fingers down his long hair. "Just a few days."

"Too long—"

"No. You needed it, my love. You're still weak. You have to stop shifting so much."

Midas sighed against the steady beat of her heart in her chest. "The mountain feels wrong," he said, causing Elowen to stiffen. "It's too still."

Her hand cupped his cheek. "You're just tired, it's nothing."

But she didn't believe it, and knew that he was too weak

to argue. She held him for a moment before the twins joined, elated that their father was finally awake. They were intelligent boys, and understood he was still weak, so they carefully curled against him as if to use the fire in their chests to reignite his.

Then came the smell of smoke that came from none of them, nor did it come from the hearth or a cooking fire.

This smoke was wrong—acrid, wild, hungry. Midas lifted his head sharply, nostrils flaring. His body ached. His limbs shook.

"Someone has found us."

Elowen stood pale and frozen. She had predicted this very thing, and her fears had become realized so soon after she was relieved to see Midas awake.

The boys looked up, their faces wide with dread.

Midas tried to stand and shift back to his beast form. He collapsed.

"I can't—" he snarled. "I can't shift again."

Elowen rushed to him, cradling his face. "Then don't. We will run. We will hide."

"No," he said. "You hide. I protect."

Metal against stone dragged against their ears: a taunt from the humans before shouts followed. Torches, steel, and armored boots closed in on their hidden home.

Midas stood at the mouth of the cave, panting, one arm braced against the wall, his chest rising and falling in shallow gasps.

He could not shift. He could feel the dragon inside him screaming—begging to rise—but there was nothing left to give. He had no heat nor strength.

Behind him, Elowen gripped the boys tightly, her voice

low and shaking. She pushed them in the opposite direction. "Go. Deep into the cave. Now."

"But—" Kalen began.

"Now!"

They flinched. Elowen had never raised her voice like that. Her eyes were wide with panic. Her hand trembled as she touched their shoulders, and for only the second time in their young lives, they saw what they hoped to never see again: fear in their parents' eyes.

"Listen to me," she said, kneeling before them. "When I find you in a moment, you stay with me. You do not leave my side. No matter what you hear."

Kalen's lip wobbled. "But Papa—"

"Your father will protect us. But our job is to stay alive, to run and hide. Do you understand?"

They nodded, tears already forming.

Elowen pushed them along and then turned to Midas, who was watching her. She stepped forward and cupped his face, kissed him hard and fast.

"I love you," she whispered. "You don't stop fighting. You hear me? We will be okay. I promise."

He nodded once. And then she turned, and disappeared into the shadows of the cave with their children. The last thing Midas heard from them was the echo of small feet retreating into darkness.

THEY CAME in fast with the reckless, violent momentum of those who sought to destroy legends once and for all. Boots struck the once serene stones of the cave. Their shadows reflected on the walls from their torches, transforming their shapes into distorted beasts of chaos with every step closer they took.

At least thirty of them—men in iron and leather, faces painted with soot, blades drawn. Some bore crossbows, others curved axes, each one marked by fear masquerading as righteousness. They had hunted beasts before, of course. They knew what it was like to corner prey. And the sight of Midas, alone and in human form, gave them confidence.

He stood protectively with his back to the deeper tunnels of the cave where his family hid. His shoulders were square despite his trembling, and his hair was wet and matted with the sweat of anxiety.

"The dragon lives in a man's skin," one said, disgusted at the sight. "Let's see how he dies in it."

Midas didn't give them the satisfaction of an answer. He simply stepped forward, pulling whatever will was buried in him to once again become the beast of legends that they feared.

He was slower. Weaker. The strain of exhaustion burned through his remaining fire like poison. It stirred his chest, but he could not reach it. He could not bring it forward. His dragon instincts shifted inside of him restlessly and furiously, exhausted beyond anything he had felt before. Every movement hurt—but he moved like a cornered creature, desperate and afraid and acting on pure instinct. He had chosen love over survival, over protection, and now he had naught but claws at the tips of his awkward human hands to defend his family with.

Steel rushed toward him. Cuts painted his fragile human skin. His heartbeat pounded with fear and his knuckles were torn down to the bone. Pain bloomed from every inch of his body, but he could not let them see him fall. He ducked beneath a blade, drove his fist into a jaw, elbowed a second man in the throat.

He fought without elegance or restraint or even reason. Blood slicked along the cavern floor from both man and beast.

But there were too many.

They adjusted. Observed his weak points in this man-flesh. They tightened their circle around him and fought on relentlessly until he was forced to his knees. White hot pain followed a crack of a whip, but he found his footing once more. He could not afford to fall.

Five of them slipped past to try and make their way deeper into the den. Midas snarled, lunging for them, arms closing around empty air as they vanished into the shadows as the others whipped and slashed and beat Midas back down to his knees.

Still, Midas didn't fall to their weapons. He could not. For hiding behind him deep in the cave lay everything he loved.

But he did not know their fate had already found them.

FORTY-SIX

After a long, bloody few minutes, Midas stopped trying to overpower the men.

Instead, he let them hurt him—allowed them to believe they had bested him. While Midas lay on the cold, blood-slicked stones of the ground, he observed the men and found their own weaknesses to use against them.

One had a slight limp. Midas slashed at the tendon at the base of his ankle. Another has a cut in his leather from Midas' claws, and he ripped through flesh with his teeth. A third was holding a sword too heavy for his skill, and Midas used the refined muscle of his tail to swipe it from his hand.

He slammed one man's head into a stalactite and used the recoil to roll beneath a swinging axe that bit the flesh of his comrade. He hooked an ankle, dragged a man off balance, and stomped down on the chest.

Pain continued to scream through Midas, but pain was survivable.

A whip wrapped his forearm, but before the man could

pull, Midas yanked him forward instead, head-butting him hard enough to crack teeth. He tore the whip free and snapped it once, twice, to create space, to make them hesitate.

That hesitation saved him.

He fought on ugly and savagely. Used spit and blood and darkness. Threw rocks into eyes. Shoved torches to flammable cloth so smoke choked the air.

By the time they realized what he was doing, it was too late for them.

They came to kill a monster.

And a monster they found.

MIDAS STUMBLED DOWN THE TUNNEL, clawing at the stone to keep upright, vision blurred with heat and desperation. His body—still human and still wrong, now injured—dragged behind the panic screaming through his soul.

"Elowen!"

No answer.

"Kalen! Auric!"

No answer.

And then the scent hit him: copper. The smell of soft flesh cooling far too fast. When Midas reached the final chamber where his family hid, he stopped. No—the *world* stopped.

Elowen lay crumpled near the wall, her body shielding both boys. One of her hands was still raised to cover their eyes, as if she'd died trying to comfort them from their fates.

Kalen was curled beneath her, unmoving, his second horn missing and blood coating his face. Auric was beneath them both, curled against Elowen's stomach as if seeking the safety of her womb.

There was only stillness.

They had been executed. Nothing more. Nothing less. A clean, *merciless* erasure of his family.

The soldiers were gone, because they didn't need to stay and gloat. They accomplished what they came to do, and left Midas to find the ashes of his failure.

Midas dropped to his knees. The cave groaned under him.

He crawled to Elowen. Touched her hair. Her cheek. Still warm, as if she were simply asleep. But he could feel the coldness taking her, stemming from the blade they left in her chest.

"Please," he said.

He lifted Kalen—his son's head lolled back, eyes open just a sliver, like he'd still been looking for him. Auric's tiny body was curled inward and limp like the others.

All three of them. Gone.

Midas made no sound at first, the shock and pain rendering him...*unfeeling*.

But then he touched Elowen again, feeling for certain that her body had grown colder, and his body flickered in anger. He shifted from the distress, the agony of the sight. It was a violent change that flung blood from his joints and left bones broken in the shift. But he did not care.

He folded his limp, aching wings around their bodies,

his entire body trembling. To feel them all there was a small blessing, for they were together again. But then Midas roared.

It cracked the stone. It shook the mountain itself, triggering an avalanche of snow and rocks that sealed the entrance of the cave from the world.

Midas did not eat. He did not move. He simply curled his massive body around his family, sheltering them from the world once more.

Day by day, Midas' fire dulled until he was as cold as them. On the last day, he opened his eyes slightly to observe the hoard before him. The gold, the jewels—it all meant nothing, for his heart was in three pieces under his wings.

In his final moments, Midas hummed to himself a song Elowen sang to the boys as babes, tears trickling down his scales as hunger and grief finished what the humans began.

And when the mountain was silent again, the last dragon was entombed in stone.

ACKNOWLEDGMENTS

Thank you so much to the readers who have continued to support my journey as an author—over the past few months your feedback has really helped me solidify my strengths and weaknesses as a writer, and I think I've finally found a flow that suits me. While some of my experimental novels haven't exactly hit the mark, I hope you could tell that I put my heart in Entombed and felt very connected to this story and these characters.

None of this would be possible if you, the reader, didn't support me with every page read, so thank you from the bottom of my heart.

Thank you to my husband for encouraging me and telling me how proud you are every day of what this career has become.

Thank you to my number one fan, my mom, for your unwavering support.

Thank you to Rilee Harris, whose Midas artwork and graphics can be found throughout the book. I don't think any artist could have done a more beautiful job in capturing the essence of this book, and I hope our professional relationship will continue for a long time as we collaborate to bring more characters to life!

Thank you to the American Foundation for Suicide Prevention for your commitment to my personal journey and your continued support.

ALSO BY
ARIEL N. ANDERSON

Under Your Scars

Delilah: An Under Your Scars Novella

Venus

King of the Damned

Queen of the Wicked

Entombed

and many more to come...

Instagram: @ariel.n.anderson